HURRICANE LAINE

By
Alex McAnders

McAnders Books

*****

Get 6 FREE ebooks and an audiobook by signing up for Alex Anders' mailing list at: AlexAndersBooks.com
Official Website: www.AlexAndersBooks.com
YouTube Channel: Bisexual Romance Author Vlog
Podcast: www.SoundsEroticPodcast.com
Visit Alex Anders
at: Facebook.com/AlexAndersBooks & Instagram

Published by McAnders Publishing

Titles by Alex McAnders

MMF Bisexual Romance

Hurricane Laine; Book 2; Book 3; Book 4

HURRICANE LAINE

Chapter 1

Jules

Do you know that feeling when you're doing everything right? You're following the rules. You're trying to be a good person and life kicks you in the ass? And I'm not talking about a friendly bump on the butt to encourage you to keep going. I'm talking about when life really pulls back its foot and lets it fly.

Maybe you don't see it coming. Maybe you don't realize what's happening until you're face down in a pile of cow dung… because in this imaginary scenario you're on a farm for some reason. But you get the point. You're just trying to do your best and live like the way everyone told you you should and life mauls you like a horny, rabid dog… that also lives on a farm.

Well, that's me now as I sit in my temporary assignment manager's office. Bill is the guy who is supposed to find me work. And he has been finding me work. Has he been finding me enough work to get by? Yes, barely.

Honestly, I can't blame Bill for where I'm at. The only thing I can blame is life. I've been working. I've been getting assignments, showing up on time, and I've been doing what they have been asking me to do.

When I'm there I'm friendly but not too friendly. I smile politely even when people make bad jokes. And I'm sure to not only learn everyone's name, but to use it in a sentence to show them that I know it.

'Yes, Aiden, that Baby Yoda meme is very funny. Yes, Brie, I did get Aiden's Baby Yoda meme. Yes, Pat, I definitely know who Baby Yoda is and I'm not just saying I do because the entire office seems obsessed with it and if I don't say I do, I'll get branded as the weird temp who will never find a husband and probably die alone.'

…Okay, that got dark, fast. But, you get my point. I'm a good temp. Yet, for whatever reason, I keep working these assignments which are supposed to be for two or three months, and less than halfway through, I'm called into Bill's office, just like I am today, to be told the same thing.

"So, Jules, I have some bad news."

"Don't say it, Bill,"

"I'm sorry. We're going to have to replace you on the assignment."

"But, why? I don't understand it. Did I do something wrong?"

"You didn't do anything wrong."

"Then, why am I being replaced?"

"It's a corporate thing."

"It's a corporate thing? What does that even mean? How is my work assignment as the invoice coordinator at a plastics company "a corporate thing"?" I asked Bill nearing my breaking point.

Bill gave me a look and then shrugged. "What can I say? I'm sorry. I just do what I'm told. But, I promise you, you didn't do anything wrong. You've been a great employee everywhere you've worked. Everyone likes you. I'm sure I'll find you something new very soon."

"But, you don't understand. I need this job. Like... mortgage and student loans. I've been taking care of my mother and..."

I stopped talking because I remembered one of the fundamental rules of temp work. No one wants to hear your problems. They have their own problems and if you want to keep working there, you have to keep your drama to yourself. These people aren't your friends. They're just under-appreciated co-workers who block out the emptiness of their lives with their obsession with memes... what, too dark again? Anyway, you get my point.

"Bill, if you can find me something ASAP, I would really appreciate it. I was counting on the money from this job."

"I promise you, as soon as something crosses my desk that you would be a fit for, I'll give you a call. I promise," Bill said sounding sincere.

"I would really appreciate that," I said trying to fight off the abyss of despair that threatened to consume me.

Getting up to go I felt my phone buzz. As I'm heading to his office door, I take out my phone. I have a text from Bill. Without opening it, I turned back to him.

"Did you just text me?"

"I did. You seem really down. I thought I'd send you something that picks me up."

I turned back to the text and opened it. It's a Baby Yoda meme. I have got to figure out where Baby Yoda is from. I'm gonna guess 'Game of Thrones'?

I thanked Bill with a polite, tight-lipped smile and left. Crossing through the open-space office looking at the eager young faces signing up for 'Temporary Temps', I couldn't help but think about how things had gone so wrong for me. This wasn't supposed to be my life.

I had a good thing going in Seattle. I had a job. I had friends. I had things to do on a Saturday night. But, then my mother got sick and I had to return home to Calabasas, California, a city whose main export are Kardashians. Yeah, it's not the place to be broke and jobless.

The great thing is that my mother is doing much better now. It was cancer. They caught it early. She's in full remission and she's just about back to normal.

The downside is that her treatment has not only destroyed her savings but has put her on medical leave from her job for months. My mother used to make a lot of money. She was… I mean, is the VP of a successful entertainment company. That's what allowed her to pay off her mortgage a few years ago.

Paying for my college tuition is what got her the second mortgage on her home. She wouldn't have had any problem paying for that too if it wasn't for all of her medical debt. And, yeah, she had insurance.

So, with her needing someone to take care of her, I left my job and Seattle and moved in with her. Finding out about her financial situation, I started looking for a job as soon as she started feeling better. Not being sure if I could live in Calabasas long term, I applied to 'Temporary Temps'. But, with them continuously yanking the rug from under me, I haven't been able to help my mother at all. Now she is at risk of losing her home.

Do you know that feeling of stomach-churning guilt because your mother took on a 2nd mortgage to pay for your education and you are the worst daughter in the world because you can't even keep a job long enough to help her, sending you into to downward spiral of hopelessness and gloom? Yeah, me neither. I was just asking for a friend.

With all of life crumbling around me at once I did what every respectable Calabasas resident would do, I got a $6 cup of coffee. Could I have found coffee cheaper elsewhere? Sure. But it wasn't about the coffee. It was about the experience of getting it. Think of it as my splurge lunch. Now that $6 seems like a bargain, right?

Sitting on the patio of the coffee shop across from Temporary Temps, I stared at the office building wondering what the hell I was supposed to do next. I couldn't keep working with them. 'They let me go because of corporate?' What does that even mean? And, how is that in any way fair?

If one day I decided to not show up for an assignment, I would get blackballed. But, they could remove me from an assignment even though, as Bill said, everyone liked me and I was doing a great job? Why was all of this happening to me?

It was as the tears made their way to my eyes that I looked around and saw someone I truly never expected to see. It was a guy I knew from college. At least I think it was. That was approaching ten years ago. And it wasn't anyone I was friends with, but I certainly saw him around campus.

We had both gone to a small, mid-western college. The school wasn't big enough to not at least recognize everyone's face. What were the odds of running into him in a coffee shop in the middle of the day in Calabasas?

Now, here's the tricky part. I recognize him, but I don't remember his name. Here's the other thing. I have put on a few pounds since college. I was never really a thin girl, so those few pounds have tipped the scales for me.

Back then I could have considered myself to be "solid". Now, I'm... how would I say this so that I'm not being horrible to myself? Now I'm pleasantly plump.

So, with all of that in mind, do I even bother striking up a conversation? What would be the point? It wasn't like we were friends.

On the other hand, I don't remember him being this good looking. It wasn't like he was a part of the sweatsuit brigade in college, but the tailored shirt he was wearing was hanging on him like a bad habit. He's the type of guy who, if I were in a better state of mind, would make me think of sex. That's worth fumbling through a forgotten name.

As to the extra 50 pounds, couldn't I tell him that it wasn't mine and I was just holding it for a friend? Sure I could. He'd believe that, right? Besides, it's not like my life could get any worse.

"I'm sorry," I said grabbing the good looking guy's attention. When he looked at me, he had this steely look in his eyes that, if I were in a better state of mind, might have made my down-below quiver. "Do I know you?"

The good looking man flashed a good looking smile. "I don't know. Do you know me?"

He said that like he was famous or something. Wait, did I actually go to school with him or do I just recognize him from TV? Freakin' Calabasas!

"No, we went to school together, didn't we? Beloit College?"

The man's face dropped recognizing the name. He stared at me trying to figure out what was going on. It took him a second, but soon his smile returned.

"Wait, yes. Yes, I know you. You used to live in... What was that dorm closest to the gym? It was our senior year," he said excitedly.

"Haven. Yeah, it was Haven. It was our senior year. You got it," I said feeling a glimmer of hope remembering a time when my life was so full of possibilities.

"That's right, Haven," he agreed with a smile. "Laine," he said offering me a wave from two tables away."

"Jules."

"That's right, Jules," he said as if he recognized my name.

Laine stared at me for a moment with a pleasant smile on his face and gestured for permission to come over.

"Please," I told him welcoming the company.

"So, Jules, what have you been up to? What are you doing in Calabasas? Do you live here?"

Here was the tricky part. What was I supposed to tell him? In these types of situations, aren't you supposed to humblebrag about the great things going on in your life? So, what was that for me? I could tell him that I recently found $10 in a pants pocket, but I didn't want to make him feel *that* jealous.

"Honestly, not much," I told him instead. "I was up in Seattle for a while. But a family situation brought me back here."

"Are you from here?" Laine asked getting better looking by the second.

"Yeah. Not Calabasas, but Southern California."

"And, where do you work? What do you do?"

He had to ask me that, didn't he? It was such an L. A. thing to ask. I didn't have the energy to blow smoke up his ass. It had already been a long day, so I told him the truth.

"I don't work anywhere, actually."

"Oh, are you married?"

I laughed. I hadn't even dated anyone since moving back here. My lady bits have already twice filed for unemployment.

"No. It's just that I've been looking for something temporary because I don't know how long my "family situation" will last, and the agency I was working through can't seem to get their act together," I said deciding it was better to blame my situation on corporate.

"Oh, okay," he replied with quickly diminishing interest. Freakin' L. A.!

"But, how about you? What have you been up to? You look like you've done well for yourself."

This was what got his focus back on me. Who would have guessed that a guy would want to talk about himself?

"Actually, I'm doing very well. I own an investment firm."

"Really?" I asked suddenly understanding what he meant by "very well".

"Yeah. After college I moved to New York to work for one of the big banks. I shorted a couple of stocks right before the great recession and then took home a fortune," he said with a million-dollar smile.

"So, when the economy was crashing?" I asked him.

"I was raking it in."

"Huh," I said as I began to consider the morality of how he made his money.

"But, don't mistake me for those asshole bankers packaging those toxic mortgages. That wasn't me."

"No, you just made money by betting on those banks to fail."

"Actually, it was by betting on them being too big to fail," he said with another smile.

It had been a long time since I had thought about back then. We were just recent graduates entering an about to be devastated job market. It wasn't something I had the energy to think about now.

"So, are you married?" I asked him trying to cut to the good bits.

"No. Not married," he told me flatly.

"Special someone?"

"Nope. Nothing."

"How?" I asked sounding like I was flirting... because I was.

"Who knows," he said with a charming smile.

Yeah, that told me everything I needed to know. He wasn't married because he didn't want to be. Clearly, he was the type that liked to keep his options open. If today was going to end in sex, I would have to remember that. Not that it was...

"I see," I said returning his smile.

"It's funny that you asked me about that," he said seeming like he wanted me to probe.

"Why?"

Laine leaned back in his seat and looked away. "You ever get yourself in a weird situation, that you don't know how you ended up in?"

"Laine, you don't know how often. I live in that state."

Laine chuckled. "Then maybe you can relate. I'm heading down to the Bahamas in about a week…"

"Nope, can't relate," I said cutting him off. He chuckled again.

"I'm heading down in about a week and I'm going to be hanging out with a friend."

"Sounds nice."

"Yeah, but I might have told the friend a bit of an exaggeration."

"What's that?"

"I told him that I was dating someone and that I would be bringing them."

"Why would you tell him that?" I asked confused.

"I don't know. He's just a guy that makes me feel… There are some people who always make you feel bad about yourself no matter how well you're doing. That's him."

Damn, how rich does his friend have to be to make a successful investment banker feel bad about himself?

"I think I know something about how that feels," I told him genuinely relating.

"Yeah, well, that's him. And, in order to not look like a total loser, I have to find someone to go with me and pretend to be my fiancé."

"Your fiancé?"

"Yeah, I know," he said lowering his head and rubbing his eyebrows in frustration.

"I gotta say, Laine, you've gotten yourself into quite a dilemma. So, are you gonna tell him the truth?"

"Oh, god no. I can't do that."

"Why not?"

Laine paused for a moment as something flashed through his mind. "I just can't do that."

"So, what are you gonna do?"

"I have to find somebody."

"You have to find someone to go to the Bahamas with you. Yeah, good luck with that," I joked.

"It's not as easy as you think," he protested.

"Really? You can't find somebody to go to the Bahamas with you?"

"No. I can't."

"I find that hard to believe."

"I can prove it," Laine said confidently.

"How?"

"Like this. Jules, would you like to go to the Bahamas with me and pretend to be my fiancé?"

"Oh, I would love to but can't. I have to work."

"See!" He said triumphant.

"Okay, I see what you mean. But the only reason I can't do it is because I have to work. Believe me, if I didn't, I would absolutely do it. I can't tell you how much I need a trip to the Bahamas right now."

"What, the family thing?" He asked becoming more serious.

"It's a money thing. I really need to work right now. I mean, I'm not gonna get into it, but I really need the money."

So you know that feeling when a suuupper rich, suuupper handsome guy is staring at you with a twinkle in his eye that makes you want to throw yourself at him like a rug? Well, that might be what's going on now.

"Why are you staring at me like that?" I asked him.

"The only thing stopping you from helping me out is money?"

"Yeah. I don't know what world you live in. But, in my world, it's a big thing."

"I'm sure. But it's something I have," he said starting to beam with confidence.

I wasn't sure how I felt about where he was going with this. "What are you suggesting?"

"How much would get you out of your "family situation"?"

"How much? Geez, I don't know. Probably more than you have."

Laine twisted his head in doubt. God was this guy cocky. How much money did he have? My family situation could have been in the millions.

"Give me a number," he said making me question what the hell was happening.

Steadying myself I looked at Laine again. How much did I remember about him from college? Not much. I think I do remember him being a little full of himself back then, too. I really didn't interact with him, but I was starting to remember female friends who did. If I remembered correctly, he was a bit of a man whore.

And, didn't I have a girlfriend who came crying to me about him? Was that about Laine or someone else? It was such a long time ago. It's hard to remember.

Whoever it was about, it had been ten years. People change. Situations change. More importantly than all of that, *my* situation had changed. And here was a guy asking me how much money I needed to get out of the hole I'm in. What do I tell him?

If his offer was real, I certainly didn't want to scare him off by saying a number that was too high. At the same time, he was bragging about having a lot of money. Why shouldn't I at least be honest?

"$200,000."

"$200,000?" He asked with a broad smile.

"Yeah. There are medical expenses involved and a student loan that…"

"Deal," he said cutting me off.

"What?" I asked sure that I had misunderstood him.

"I said it's a deal. I'll do it. If you come with me to the Bahamas and pretend to be my fiancé, I'll pay you $200,000."

I was stunned. There was no way he couldn't tell. He was just looking at me with this cocky grin on his face and I didn't know how I felt about it. What had I gotten myself into? For some reason, I felt like a mouse who had been cornered by a cat.

Why should I feel that way, though? Laine wasn't a cat, he was my savior. That number would cover what my mother had borrowed to send me to school. It wouldn't wipe away her medical debt, but it would pay off her mortgage and give her the breathing room needed between now and when she would be able to return to work.

It wasn't a million dollars, but this was not-being-kicked-out-of-our-home money. This would allow me to return to the way things were before all hell broke loose. Could this really be happening?

"Half up front," I suddenly said.

"What?" he replied caught off guard.

"I would need half of it before I left," I explained to him.

He looked at me regathering his self-assuredness. "And how do I know you won't just take the money and disappear on me?"

"How do I know you'll pay me in the end? How do I know if you even have that type of money?"

Laine laughed as if I was ridiculous for suggesting such a thing. How much money did this guy have?

"Tell you what," Laine began while pulling a card out of his pocket. "I would love to talk to you about this some more, but maybe we should both do a little research on each other before we commit to something fully. Here's my card. Look me up and let me know tomorrow. If you get a better offer between then and now, I understand. Otherwise, I'm really happy I ran into you and you will love my private island."

With that, Laine pushed his business card in front of me, got up, and headed towards the most expensive car I'd ever seen. I think it was a Jaguar, but it was the type that required a British accent when you said it. I'm not a car girl, but that thing was nice.

Hearing his engine roar and watching him drive off, I next looked down at his card. It read, 'Laine Toro, Triad Investments.' Typing that into my phone his picture was the first thing to come up. It turned out, he hadn't been exaggerating. He was insanely rich.

His company had 5 billion dollars under management. It was clear why he laughed when I suggested that he might not have the money. If he dropped a hundred dollar bill, it wouldn't be worth his time to pick it up.

And, did he say that he had a private island in the Bahamas? Could all of this be real? Didn't there have to be some sort of catch?

"Will you have to have sex with him?" My mother asked me disturbed.

"*Have* to?"

"Yes. Will he make you have sex with him?"

"*Make* me?" I asked her as I pulled out my phone and showed her a picture of him.

My mother stared silently at Laine's picture undoubtedly weighing the morals around prostitution when it was with the hottest guy in the world.

"He seems very nice," my mother said clearly getting a full accounting of his personality from the shirtless picture I showed her. "But, what do you know about him?"

"I mean, I went to college for four years with him."

"So, you were friends in college?"

"No. But I remember him. He knew a number of my friends." And, by that, I meant that he slept with them.

"And they would vouch for him?"

"I guess." And, by that, I meant that they would say that he was a dog.

But I couldn't tell my mother that. She'd just get worried and tell me that I shouldn't do this. But I had to do this. She was months late on her mortgage payments. An eviction notice could be coming any day. I needed to do this.

And, if I end up sleeping with the hottest, most eligible bachelor in the universe while doing it, well, I guess that was a grenade I was willing to fall on. Look at me taking one for the team. I'm practically a saint.

I will admit, that his reputation from back then and the way he smiled when I asked him why he wasn't married, did worry me a bit. The last thing I wanted was to get emotionally involved with a guy who was incapable of reciprocating it. Been there. Done that. Bought the t-shirt… and then burned it along with the football jersey which he clearly loved more than me. Long story.

But, Laine wasn't asking for any of that. All he was looking for was someone to pretend to be his fiancé for a week or two to impress his billionaire friend. I wouldn't mind draping myself over him for a few weeks. And as long as I keep telling myself that this is a job, and that everything I'm doing is pretend, then I'm not gonna catch feelings.

I'm not one of those girls who fall for the first smokin' hot billionaire who has probably changed a lot since college and now has a smile that makes you want to throw yourself at. No, that's not me. And, honestly, I feel sorry for those girls.

"Hi, Laine? This is Jules. We met today at the coffee shop. Actually, we met back in college. We re-met at the coffee shop… today… in Calabasas." Keep it together Jules.

Laine laughed. "Yes, I remember. Have you given any thought to my offer?"

"I have and… no." Wait, what did I just say?

"Did you say no?"

Did I just say no? "Yeah, no," I repeated not recognizing the self-destructive crazy person who had taken control of my mouth. "It's a very generous offer. And, I definitely need the money. I mean, I really need the money. But, it just seems too weird."

"What do you mean? It's just a guy you haven't seen in ten years offering you $200,000 to pretend to be his fiancé to impress his friend. What's weird about it?"

"Are you joking? That. All of that."

Laine chuckled on the other end of the phone. "Listen, I get it. It is weird. It's all weird. And that's why I've had such a hard time finding someone to do it for me. I'm sorry I bothered you with it. Have a good life."

"Wait, is that it?" I said not liking anything about what just happened.

"What do you mean?"

"I mean, are you just gonna give up?"

"What did you want me to do?" Laine asked sounding reasonably confused.

"I don't know. You could try and convince me that it wouldn't be weird," I told him even though I really felt that I shouldn't have had too.

Laine laughed again. "Okay. Why do you think it might be weird?"

"I don't know. It's just a lot of money for just pretending."

"It's the amount you asked for."

"Yeah, but... like... when you say that I have to pretend to be your fiancé, what exactly does that involve?"

"Are you asking if I will be expecting you to have sex with me?"

"Of course I'm asking you if you are expecting me to have sex with you. What else could this be about?"

Laine chuckled again. "Just so we're clear, I'm not expecting you to have sex with me. What I need is for you to make my friend think that you are legitimately my fiancé. That pretending ends once we are alone in the bedroom."

"So, we'll be sharing a room?"

"Of course. What engaged couple doesn't share a bedroom?"

"And... will there be... how do I say this?"

"Two beds?"

"Yes. What will our sleeping arrangements be?"

"There will be one bed. If you prefer, I can sleep on the floor. Would me sleeping on the floor make it less weird for you?"

"I mean, it would. But then you would be sleeping on the floor on your own private island. That would be weird on its own."

"Then, how would you like to handle it?"

"How about we keep the floor as an option, but we play it by ear?" I told him trying to be practical.

"That seems like a reasonable compromise. Is there anything else that you want to talk about?"

"No. I think that's it."

"So, does that mean that you'll do it?" Laine asked casually.

"I guess. Yeah, sure, I'll do it."

"And, are you okay with being paid afterward?"

I thought about that part of it again. "Well, I checked you out. You seem to be good for it."

"So, is that a yes as well?"

"Yeah, sure," I said not recognizing the crazy person who had once again taken control of my mouth.

"Wonderful."

"But I do have one other question?"

"What's that?"

"Why do articles refer to you as Hurricane Laine?"

Laine laughed. "It has to do with an acquisition I made a few years ago. Sometimes when you take control of a company, you have to shake things up. I shook, and ruffled a few feathers. Ever since then, the press has taken to calling me that. I don't know, I kind of like it. It makes me seem exciting. Don't you think?"

"It definitely does," I told him in response to his perfectly reasonable explanation.

"Anything else?"

"Yeah, one other thing. How long are we gonna be there?"

"I don't know. But I would say, plan like you're going to be there for three weeks. Actually, make it a month. It may end up only being a week. It will all depend on how things go with my friend."

"What do you mean?"

"Just plan for a month. If it's shorter, it's shorter."

"Okay. And when do we leave?"

"I actually spoke to my friend today. Can you leave in three days?"

"Three days? I thought you said we'd leave in a week or more?"

"I did. But things move fast. Can you do it?"

"Umm... Yeah. Sure, I can do it."

"Great. I'll have my assistant send you the itinerary. Thanks for doing this for me. You're helping me out a lot."

"And you're helping me out a lot. It's a pleasure doing business with you."

"Yes, it's a pleasure," he said allowing his sexy smile to echo through the phone.

Hanging up I felt a lot better about everything. He had clearly changed since college. This couldn't be the same guy my friends cried on my shoulder about. Or, maybe the things from back then weren't actually his fault.

I'll admit, I was a little wilder back then. It wasn't anything over the top. But my friends were all bat shit nuts. They were fun, and I loved them, but their role model was a singer who had set her boyfriend's house on fire. It seemed reasonable at the time, but looking back on it, yikes.

So, maybe Laine wasn't as bad as I remember him to be. Maybe he just got a bad rap. And, even if he wasn't the best guy back then, who was at their best in college? Certainly not me. We're all different people now. All of us deserve a fresh start. And, with the money I'll earn from this job, I'll be able to afford one.

With me leaving in three days, there were a lot of things that I had to do. The great thing was that on top of the $200,000, Laine was giving me what I referred to as a billionaire's girlfriend allowance. It was $2000 that I could use to transform myself into someone who looked like they were dating a billionaire. Nails, hair, plucking, waxing, you know, the usual stuff. Then there was my wardrobe.

I went shopping in Beverly Hills to really play the part. There was a bikini there that cost $800. $800! So, then I drove to this little French boutique called Targét. I picked up four swimsuits and snacks for less than $200. That's right, $200! Come @ me… which I think is a thing people say.

It was the day before we were scheduled to leave that I was sent our backstory. Apparently, he and I had only met four months ago. Clearly, it was love at first sight. He flew me to Paris last week and asked me to marry him. Our imaginary engagement was so romantic. However, I'll have you know that my imaginary jetlag? It's been horrible.

Not having seen or spoken to Laine in the three days leading up to our trip, I was expecting to see him in the car he sent to pick me up. I didn't. I was then expecting to meet him for check-in. He wasn't there. In fact, I didn't even see him during my flight to Florida. I gotta say, if this was any indication of how our imaginary marriage was going to be, this pretend engagement wasn't going to last.

It wasn't until I was nervously about to board my flight to Bimini that I got a text from him. It said, "Hey Honey, I can't wait to see you at the airport. You're going to love the island."

The text set my mind at ease. This wasn't actually a new version of survivor where billionaires led unsuspecting women to a tropical island where they had to battle each other for food and $200,000. I'm not saying I wouldn't do it… and win. I'm saying, I just did my nails… so, bring it on bitches!

Approaching the island I looked down at the water. I had never been to the Bahamas. I'd seen pictures, but they didn't prepare me for this. It was beautiful. I hadn't realized those shades of blue existed.

And, the closer we got to the island, the more I was sure I could see fish swimming in the crystal clear water.

That did mean that the fish had to be larger than I felt comfortable swimming with. And that my bikini might never touch the ocean. But, the sight itself was beautiful.

Landing on the very short runway, I was relieved to be on solid ground again. When the door of the plane opened, I was surprised by how warm it was. I guess it was less the heat than the humidity, but still, it was a shock. I started sweating immediately. It wasn't a good look on me. Girls my size weren't built for such weather.

Crossing the runway and entering the small airport, I kept expecting to see Laine. All of this was new to me. Except for the imaginary trip for my engagement, I hadn't even left the country before this. I wasn't sure what I was supposed to do. I mean, the airport wasn't very big so there weren't too many places to go. But still.

Following the person in front of me, I crossed the tarmac into a small building. It wasn't very ceremonious. Come on, didn't anyone know who my pretend fiancé was? He could pretend to buy and sell this place. I don't mean to pretend to be that type of person. But, it would've been nice if crossing the airport I wasn't made to feel like the lead male character in every sitcom, you know, clueless and playing way out of my league.

"Jules, Honey, you made it!" I heard a familiar voice say.

Looking around as I stepped out of the other side of the small building, I spotted him. Laine was no longer dressed like a stylish power player. He was dressed like a guy on a yacht in a cologne commercial. He was wearing a loose-fitting white linen shirt with white khaki shorts and light brown leather sandals. Damn, did he look good.

Immediately dropping my bags I ran over to him, threw my arms around him, and gave him a kiss. The move was playful and sexy. It was what I once saw Julia Roberts do in a movie.

"Laine, dear, so good to see you," I said in a spot-on English accent.

Laine gave me a look as if he was questioning my character choice and then waved his hand towards the guy standing next to him.

"Jules, I would like you to meet Reed. Actually, Reed went to college with us."

I turned to the surprised man standing next to Laine and froze. He was more than just familiar. I knew Reed. I knew him much more than I knew Laine. In fact, he and I had a history…. a long, complicated history.

Is this a coincidence? Did Laine not know that Reed and I knew each other back then? It has to be a coincidence…, right?

Chapter 2

Reed

There is no way this is a coincidence. Three days ago Laine called me up and told me that I had to drop everything because there was someone who I had to meet. I asked him who it was, and he told me that it was his fiancé.

Laine Toros was engaged? No way. Uh-uh. Laine goes through women like tick tacks. He doesn't see them as people. To him, they're just mountains to summit. And I told him that.

But he said that this one was different. That she was special and that she turned his ways around. He said that she made him a new person. Now, come to find out that the woman who he is set to marry is the very woman who I was hopeless in love with in college. In no universe was this a coincidence.

"Reed, I'd like you to meet Jules, my fiancé," Laine said casually as if I wouldn't know who she was.

"No, we've met, Laine," I said still recovering from the shock. "I mean, we've met, right?" I asked Jules suddenly flooded by memories of our complicated past.

"No, we've definitely met," Jules clarified.

"Oh wait. That's right. You guys have met. Right!" Laine said as if all of it was coming rushing back to him. "Isn't this a small world," he continued flashing one of his annoying smiles and wrapping his arms around Jules's shoulder. "Honey, was the flight okay. I don't have to buy and sell anywhere for you, do I?"

"Oh, it's funny that you would say that," Jules said returning her gaze to Laine.

"Why?" Laine asked.

Jules smiled. "Nothing. It's just funny. So, Reed, how have you been? It's been a while. We haven't spoken since graduation day."

"You remember that?" I asked surprised that she would remember something so forgettable.

"Of course. You had put all of those polka-dot things on your gown. I always wondered, how did you do that? Was it staples?"

"Yeah!" I said shocked that she would remember something so minuscule. "It was staples. I had spent the entire night running around with... actually, it was with your fiancé here."

"I remember that," Laine said gripping Jules tighter. "You just had to add your polka-dots. You couldn't graduate without your polka-dots."

As Laine talked about it, I was reminded of that night. "You broke into that closet in the science hall to get staples, didn't you?"

"You were threatening not to walk if you didn't have your polka-dots. What was I supposed to do?" Laine reminded me.

"That's right," I said having completely forgotten that Laine could have a sweet side.

"Anyway, we have plenty of time to reminisce when we get to the island. Reed, you wouldn't mind grabbing Jules's bags, would you? Jules, is this all you brought?"

"You know how I like to travel light?"

"Yes, of course, Honey. And that's one of the things that I love about you," Laine said before touching his nose to Jules's and giving her a kiss.

Watching the two of them, I wasn't sure what was going on, but I was sure that I didn't like it. This could not be a coincidence. And there was no way that Laine had forgotten the way I had felt about her.

I couldn't count the number of times I had talked to him about her back then. I could remember us once talking about her until the sun rose. I guess I was the one doing most of the talking, but still, he couldn't have forgotten that.

"So, how did you two meet?" I asked as I drove them back to my place.

"Did Laine not tell you?" Jules asked me from the back of the golf cart.

"No. In fact, Laine hasn't told me anything about you two."

"Shame on you Laine. Dear, let me."

"It's all yours, Honey."

"We were both in Calabasas…"

"I have a home up there," Laine said smugly.

"He does. And I recently moved back to take care of my mother."

"Oh, what was wrong with your mother?" I asked concerned.

"Cancer treatment. But, she's in full remission. Everything's fine."

"Your mother had cancer? I didn't know that?" Laine interjected.

"Of course you did. I told you that. You knew I moved back to Calabasas to care for my mother."

"Oh wait. Yes, to care for your mother. Of course. You know what, I was thinking of someone else. Anyway, go on."

"Anyway," Jules continued, "I was working at a temp agency…"

"A temp agency?" I asked her suddenly reminded of something.

"Yeah. Not knowing how long I would be there, I thought it would be easier. In either case, I had just been fired from another temp assignment when I decided to go have a coffee. And, wouldn't you know it, who was at the same coffee shop? Laine Toros, from college."

"It was me," Laine said chiming in. "Then, one thing led to another, we started talking, and here we are."

"Here we are," Jules confirmed.

"Wow! I don't believe that things like that just happen," I told them. "I guess you two were meant to be."

"We were meant to be," Laine said slipping Jules's hand into his own.

Seeing yet another of their displays of affection, I returned my attention to the narrow, empty street. This was a lot to take in. It took me a long time to get over Jules. In fact, she was one of the reasons I had moved here after college.

The whole thing with her really messed with my head. I don't know why I couldn't get myself to just ask her out. I had always felt like she would have said yes if I had, but I never did. I'm not sure why I didn't. Maybe I was just too screwed up back then. Hell, maybe I'm still screwed up.

I mean, what have I even done with my life while Laine has been out making himself richer than god? Nothing. I'm living in the same broken-down house I moved into ten years ago when I got here, and I still barely have a penny to my name.

Seeing the Johnsons wave at me as I approached, I waved back and made note that I had to stop by their place and say hi when I got back on the island. They were getting up in age and there were a couple of us who kept up their yard for them. My turn was coming up soon.

"Mr. and Mrs. Johnson, how's Thelma and your new grandbaby doing?"

"She doin' just fine," Mr. Johnson said after I pulled over next to him.

"Do you know if she got those mangos I left for her?"

"Ya know, I think she did."

"That's good. They were very sweet. I'll have to bring you some."

"You know we always like your mangos," Mr. Johnson said with a smile.

"By the way, these are a couple of friends of mine. They're visiting from the States. You remember me talking about Laine. And this is his Fiancé, Jules. We all went to college together."

"Very nice to meet you, sir," Mr. Johnson said to Laine before turning to me. "Is this the girl you talk about?"

"Oh, I'm sure I don't know what you mean. Anyway, I'll bring those mangos by. I'll see you when I get back," I said pulling off before Mr. Johnson could say another word.

Yes, I had mentioned Jules and my heartache about her many times to them over the years. And now that Mr. Johnson was getting up there in age, his filter wasn't what it used to be. There was nothing about what he would say that I would want to have to explain.

"They seemed very nice," Jules said again grabbing my attention.

"Yes. Everyone's very nice here. It's a small community so everyone knows each other. I'm the godfather to their grandson," I said proudly.

"You mean Thelma's son?" She said as if she knew who she was talking about. "Thelma with the mangos."

I laughed. "Yes, Thelma with the mangos."

"It's a quaint little island," Laine said deliberately cutting us off.

At least once a year Laine came down to visit. He clearly didn't get island life. It was too working class for him. He never talked after I introduced him to someone. And I always got the impression that he resented me being here. So when he told me that he had bought an island a few miles off the coast of South Bimini, I was more than a little stunned.

He hadn't even mentioned it to me until his call three days ago. He had to have come down to visit it at some point before buying it, didn't he? Or did people like him buy million-dollar homes sight unseen? I mean, my place had to be a dump in comparison to his and I walked through it five times before buying it.

"We're here," I announced as we pulled up to my humble home.

When I looked back at Jules, I found her staring at my house surprised.

"Something wrong?" I asked her suddenly feeling self-conscious.

"No. I just had the impression that… Do you not do what Laine does… job-wise?"

"Oh no. God no," I joked.

"You don't have to say it like that," Laine replied with a smile.

"No, I think one person doing what Laine does is enough. The world only has so many companies to exploit. Right, Laine?" I said giving him a gentle ribbing.

"Of course, otherwise I would be a lot richer. No, Reed here followed his own path."

"Oh, what do you do?" Jules asked.

"A little of this. A little of that. Mostly I run an after school program where I offer college prep classes. It's not really a paid thing, but it's what I can do. So… you know."

"He's been running it for five years," Laine added. "Hey Reed, tell her how many kids you've gotten to go off to college."

"Six," I said proudly.

"Yeah, that's almost one a year… After five years," Laine said with his usual level of contempt for what I do.

"Actually, this year we have two."

"Two whole students, huh?"

I turned to Jules. "In the ten years before I started the program, only one person had gone to college, so those numbers are a big deal here."

"No, that sounds amazing," Jules said sincerely.

"Thank you!" I said kinda having to hold back a tear.

Back in college, Jules and I never had an in-depth conversation. In fact, I thought she was a bit of a party girl. I couldn't imagine college-Jules appreciating the simpler things in life. Considering who she was engaged to, maybe she still doesn't. But, damn would it be hard for a guy not to fall for a girl who says things like that.

Laine interrupted my lingering gaze at his fiancé by pushing her out of the golf cart and guiding her towards my front door. "So, Jules, what do you think of Reed's place?"

Jules turned from me to Laine and the small, one-bedroom, dusty, orange home in front of her. "It's… nice," she said clearly being polite.

"Yep, $150,000 in tuition and this is what it got him," Laine said mockingly.

I didn't say anything to that because I was used to him making such cracks. But, I gotta say, I hated that he was now saying it in front of Jules.

"How glad are your parents that they spent the money?" Laine said with an asshole smirk.

"He's changing people's lives. I'm sure they're very happy they spent the money," Jules quickly replied.

Laine's smile shifted a little as he stared at his fiancé. The two were staring at each other with weird looks on their faces. It was like they were sizing each other up. What was going on here? Whatever it was, I was liking Jules more by the second.

"Honey, can I speak to you for a moment," Laine asked her making me feel a little awkward.

"Sure, Dear," she replied seeming to not back down.

"Hey Reed, why don't you grab our bags. There's no need to hang around here. We'll just go to the boat and head over to the island."

"You got it, sir. And, while I'm at it, I'll give your shoes a quick shine," I said letting him know that he was being a bit of a prick again.

"Yeah, whatever," Laine said dismissively.

Laine and Jules walked towards the street without saying a word. It felt like they were waiting for me to leave, so I did. Entering the house, I thought about the unlikeliness of this all. How was it that out of all of the people in the world, Laine had ended up with the one woman who was seared into my brain, and who I had never gotten over? Sure, I had moved on from her, but that wasn't the same thing.

I would say that it was torture seeing her again, except for the fact that it wasn't. It was wonderful seeing her again. She was as beautiful as she had ever been and now I was discovering a side to her that was hard to describe, but that I definitely liked.

Crossing into the bedroom, I navigated the small space. It still amazed me that Laine was willing to sleep here when he could so easily afford a hotel room. Sure, it made sense that he would stay with me. Visiting me was the only purpose of his trip.

But he clearly had so much contempt for everything about my life and the way I lived. Why would he subject himself to it? And, mine was only a full-sized bed. We were practically sleeping on top of each other.

I was fine with it. We had shared enough beds in college that I was used to it. But he couldn't be. I had never seen it, but I was sure he slept on the largest bed there was. Laine liked to have the best of everything. So, his bed probably cost more than my whole house.

That was always what made his visits so unusual. He clearly didn't appreciate the people here, and he was judgmental about the way I lived and what I did. Yet, every year he came to see me and slept on my cramped bed when he did.

This was why I forgave him for the little cracks he made. In spite of it all, he really was still a friend. In fact, past the people on the island, he was my only friend. And, I really did care about him. His life had become unrecognizable to me. And he had clearly made some questionable decisions which probably ended up hurting a lot of people. But, he was my best friend.

He was the guy who had listened for hours as I went on and on about Jules. He was the guy who, when classes and exams became overwhelming for me, would wrap his arm around my shoulder and tell me I could do it. In college, I couldn't have imagined having a better friend than Laine. It was the person he had turned into since then who I had my doubts about.

But, that compassionate guy still had to be in there somewhere. Behind the hurtful swipes at my life choices and heartless corporate raiding, had to be the guy who had always been there for me. The guy who broke into a locked closet to get me staples so that I could attach polka-dots to my graduation gown, still had to be in there, right?

That sweet guy was always the person I hoped would walk off of the plane every time he arrived. Yet, for whatever reason, that guy never showed up. And honestly, this new guy was not always fun to be around. In fact, it is safe to say that he was often one asshole-comment away from me hating him.

"Reed, are we going? Or, are we just gonna stay here with our thumbs up our ass?" Laine said from the front door.

Returning to the present, I looked down at his designer leather bags and the canvas duffel bag I had since college. "You could help, you know?"

"Of course I could. But I didn't want to rob you of the joy of slaving for others. I know how you love that."

I could hear Laine cross the small living room towards me. He entered the bedroom and grabbed his bags.

"Is that what you think I do? Slave for others?"

"Let's see, you work and don't get paid for it. What do you think being a slave is?"

"I get paid," I retorted.

"In what? Mangos?"

"In thanks," I tried to explain to him.

"In thanks?" Laine laughed. "I'll offer that option instead the next time I need to do layoffs. I'll tell them that it isn't that that I'm firing them. It's that from now on, I'll be paying them in thanks. I'm sure everyone will be on board with that."

"You know, you could be a real dick some times," I told him unable to hold it back.

"Yeah, well, you can be an idiot. So, I guess we're the perfect pair," Laine said with a smug smile.

With his bags in hand, Laine crossed back through the house and exited. Grabbing my bag I questioned whether or not I should even go through with the trip. Was Laine's friendship really still worth it? It had been ten years since the good times. In reality, could he seriously still be considered a friend? Was his abuse worth it?

"Reed?" I heard Jules say from the living room.

Grabbing my bag I went out to meet her. Her eyes were slowly scanning the unimpressive room.

"Hey, what's up?"

Her eyes flicked to mine. "I was just wondering if I could get some water."

"Oh sure. Yeah," I said resting down my bag and heading to the fridge. "I'm sorry I didn't offer you any before."

"No. That's fine. And, I'm sorry about Laine."

"What?" I said turning towards her as I filled a glass with water.

"Laine. I'm sorry about him. I've never seen this side of him before. He can be a bit of an asshole."

I laughed. "Laine? No. He's a great guy. I'm sure he'll make a good husband."

"Husband? Oh yeah. I'm sure he'll be great. But, how have you been? This is a different kind of life. You were born in Chicago, weren't you?"

"Yeah, good memory. Evanston. It's a suburb just north of Chicago. How did you remember that?"

"I don't know. I guess you remember the important things. Listen, I didn't know that you were the friend that Laine was bringing me to meet."

"That's okay. He didn't tell you?"

"No. He just said a friend."

"Yeah, he didn't tell me it was you either."

"I guess he didn't know we knew each other," Jules suggested.

"Yeah, maybe that's it," I told her having a hard time believing it.

"But, it's really good to see you."

"Yeah, same."

"I always felt like we left things incomplete, somehow," Jules suggested.

"Yeah?" I asked unsure of what I was hearing.

"Yeah. Didn't you?"

"I mean…"

"You guys coming?"

Laine's booming voice startled me causing me to spill the water. "Oh, I'm sorry. Did I get that on you?"

"No, you missed," she said with a smile.

I handed her the glass and quickly dried the floor. After taking a few sips she handed me the glass and headed outside.

What was going on there? I was never very good with women. And my near celibacy since moving here hadn't helped. But, I was sure that I was feeling some sort of chemistry between us.

That couldn't be what was happening, though. She was Laine's fiancé. She was obviously in love with Laine. No, I had to be misreading things.

Putting the glass in the sink, I grabbed my bag, exited the house, and locked the door behind me. Keeping my eyes lowered, I allowed them to bounce up to Jules. When I did, I found her looking back. There was definitely something going on between us. And, as if being summoned from the depths, I felt my feelings for her slowly reemerge.

"So, Reed hasn't seen my island yet either," Laine explained to Jules.

"You haven't, Reed?" Jules asked.

"No. He didn't even tell me about it."

"I wanted it to be a surprise."

"You're definitely full of surprises," I told him.

"That, I am. So, I bought the island as is, which means that it came with a speed boat."

"You know how to drive a speed boat?" I asked him.

"Not yet. Luckily, the island also came with a driver."

"You have a captain?" I asked him.

"That's right, a captain. It also came with a grounds crew, housekeeper, and chef," he said proudly.

"With a staff like that, I can see why you need a captain," I told him.

"What do you mean?" Jules asked.

"Well, I assume they don't live on the island, do they?" I asked Laine.

"No."

"Right. So you need someone who will shuttle people back and forth."

"Makes sense," Jules confirmed.

"Yeah, I guess it does," Laine said with a chuckle. "But, the speed boat's mine. I think that's what I was told. 24-hour access. That's what the website said. So, what do you think? Want to do some fishing?"

Hearing that, I looked at Laine who was again sitting in the back seat as if I were his chauffeur. "You really haven't been to the island yet?"

"Nope. I bought it sight unseen. My agent visited it. He finds all of my properties. I trust his taste," Laine said with a smile.

My instinct was to shake my head in disapproval. I resisted the urge. There was no point in antagonizing Laine now. Because of Jules, I was suddenly looking forward to the stay. I probably shouldn't be, but I was.

It was a short trip from my place to the dock. When we got there, there was a slightly older guy to meet us. He wasn't someone I recognized so I figured that he was from North Bimini. That was a separate island.

"Good mornin'," the guy said in an unmistakable Bahamian dialect.

"Are you my captain?" Laine asked heading towards him.

"Mr. Toros?"

"Yes."

"Then, that's me, sir."

"Excellent. Those are our bags."

So cringy! Was that the way Laine treated people now? I really thought he said things like that to me as a joke. But, apparently not. Apparently, that was the way he talked to the help. And I guess to him, I was just the help.

"No, I got it," I said to the captain when he tried to place my bag on the cart he had retrieved. "I'm sorry, what's your name?"

"Monty."

"Reed," I said offering him my hand. "Nice to meet you."

Monty gave me a genuine smile realizing he was meeting a fellow human being. "Good to meet you, too."

"Listen, Monty, I'm gonna apologize for my friend now. He's lost touch a little."

"Don't worry, I used to it. I bin working for the owner of the house for a long time."

"I'm guessing it was a rental house?"

"Oh yeah. I can't tell you how many famous people have stayed d'ear. You name it and I've driven dem. Do you know Kim Kardashian?"

"I don't. Who's that?"

"I think she's a model. Small girl. She and her husband were the last ones there. Someone said he was a famous rapper."

"I'm not up on celebrities," I told Monty.

"Me neither. Dey all just people."

"Exactly," I told him. "But, again, I apologize for my friend."

Monty smiled. "You good people."

I don't know if I had apologized enough for what Laine would probably put him through, but it seemed like Monty got it. Everyone on Bimini usually got it. Bimini had a population of 2000 and would get ten times that number in tourists every year. Bimini was known worldwide for its sport fishing. And considering that it took less than 30 minutes to get here from Miami, the island got all types.

Following Monty and the cart full of bags, I looked ahead to see Laine and Jules standing on the dock up ahead. Laine was standing next to her with his arm around her shoulder. They made an awkward couple. It could just be me wanting to see something that wasn't there, but, from where I stood, it sure looked like she wasn't that into him.

I knew that was crazy, though. She had agreed to marry him. And the fact that Laine was willing to settle down with anyone at all had to say something about the way he felt about her. I had never thought of Laine as the marrying type. So, the fact that those two were engaged was still blowing my mind.

We all got onto Laine's new speed boat. With Monty behind the wheel, we headed out to sea. On land, it had been warm, but with the cool sea breeze blowing over us, the weather was perfect.

Although Laine talked from the moment we pulled away from the dock, I didn't say much. I was too busy processing how I felt about Jules. I had worked so hard to get her out of my mind. How did I feel now that she was back?

Every so often I would look over at her. She always caught me looking and would stare back. Her gaze was doing something to me. My chest tingled as I thought about her. And when I momentarily lost control of my thoughts and I pictured her in a bikini, I experienced a shortness of breath.

It was suddenly clear that I shouldn't have come on this trip with Laine and his new fiancé. But, the truth was that I wouldn't have had the strength to say no, even if he would have told me she would be there. I was quickly falling for her again, and I was falling hard.

Doing what I could to take my mind off of Jules, I instead focused on what Laine was saying.

"And, that's how I made my first million," I heard him say to Monty and Jules.

"Jules, did Laine ever tell you about our first Thanksgiving together?" I asked her suddenly remember the story.

"He hasn't. Actually, he hasn't told any of his stories about you two."

"Why would you bring that up?" Laine asked me genuinely confused.

"What? I wanna hear it," Jules said leaning forward to look across Laine's chest at me.

"There's no story. I invited him over to my house for Thanksgiving freshman year. We had turkey. The end."

"Seriously, is that how you remember it?" I asked.

"Yeah. What else was there to it?"

"More than that." I looked over at Jules getting comfortable in her eyes.

"So, it's freshman year, we're finishing up our midterms, it's about to be Thanksgiving and I really didn't want to go home."

"Why didn't you want to go home?" Jules interjected.

"His father's a judge," Laine told her.

"Your father's a judge?"

"Yeah," I confirmed.

"Wow! Okay. But what does that have to do with why you didn't want to go home?"

"He was a judge in all ways. He was a pretty judgmental guy. He was never happy with any of my choices. Anyway, I really didn't want to go home and I told Laine that. Laine insisted I have Thanksgiving at his place."

"I don't know why I did that."

"So, I go home with him, but what he didn't tell me was that his house had two things, beds and a floor.

And he didn't even have a big bed. So for the entire weekend, we end up squeezing onto this tiny little twin."

Laine looked down embarrassed. "I don't know why I was so insistent."

"No. I'm glad you were. So, his mother made dinner. It was so good. And before we ate, we all had to stand around the table and say what we were grateful for. I think his mother said that she was grateful to have him there for Thanksgiving. I said that I was grateful to be there. And he said that he was grateful for the Mercedes XJ5 or something."

Jules laughed.

"It wasn't exactly in the theme of the moment, but, you know, there you go. That's the man you're marrying."

"First of all, the XJ series is the Jaguar line."

Jules and I broke into laughter.

"Second of all, why would you tell that story?" Laine asked looking genuinely upset.

"What? It's a cute story. And after we had dinner, his mother had us put the leftovers onto individual plates and hand it out to the homeless. I never forgot that. That helped shape me into who I am."

"If that was what turned you into who you are, then I guess I should sincerely apologize for inviting you."

Jules snapped. "Laine, that's not nice."

Laine chuckled. "What? I'm joking. He knows I'm joking. We have fun like that."

"Well, I thought it was a good story," Jules confirmed. "Thanks for the insight," she said with a wink.

I looked at Jules's empathetic face and then at the asshole bastard sitting next to me. The contrast between the two was...

Wow! Do you know that feeling when someone goes one joke too far, and after years and years of taking their shit, you finally... hit your limit? I think I do. I really think I do.

Was what Laine had just said any worse than everything else he had said over the years? No, probably not, but... Wow! I really think that I've finally taken all I can take from him.

It's weird, I didn't even feel that upset by what he had said... Okay, maybe that's not true. Maybe I'm super pissed. How dare he shit on me like this in front of Jules? What the fuck, Laine? You know what? Fuck you too! Seriously, fuck... you..., Laine! I'm done with you!

Keeping a composed look on the outside, I wondered how I should respond. Should I insist that Monty turn the boat around? Should I go to the island, stay for the day and then head back with the staff?

I looked over at Jules and caught her eyes. She smiled at me. She was a woman I had been in love with all throughout college and for years after. Now, here she was back in my life. Do I walk away from that? Why would I do that? Out of loyalty to Laine? Why? What had he done in the past 10 years that made him deserving of such loyalty? No, serious, in 10 years, what had he done?

And didn't he just spring her on me as if I wouldn't have feelings about it? There was no possible way in this universe that he didn't remember how I felt about her in college. And, knowing him, it was probably the reason he was interested in her in the first place.

The way I saw it, I officially owed him nothing. Which meant that Jules, the woman I had loved forever... Well, she's... no longer off-limits.

"We here," Monty announced as we pulled closer to the island in front of us.

"This is it," Laine said turning to me. "If you gotta live the island life, this is the way it should be done."

I stared at the island as we approached. Damn, was this place beautiful! Ahead of us was a dock with a smaller motorboat tied to it. Behind it to the right was a dry boat dock, I'm assuming to have a place to put the speed boat during storms. Parked on the side of it was a golf cart. And past the four hundred foot road leading away from it was the most beautiful island home I had ever seen.

It sat on a slight hill so it loomed over the sea impressively. It was painted a sky blue and its windows and doors were aligned giving the house a face. The expression was stately. The place had to be two and a half stories tall and was reminiscent of a plantation home. It was impressive.

"Well, Reed, what do you think?" Laine asked me breaking the spell the place had on me.

"It's nice," I said refusing to give him anything that would feed his inflated sense of self-importance.

"That's it? Nice?" Laine said uncharacteristically upset.

"Yeah, what else do you want me to say? It's nice."

"Really, Reed? Hey, Jules, what do you think of my new home?"

I turned to Jules for the first time since we arrived. She was staring at the place awestruck. Closing her mouth, she turned to Laine. "It's amazing."

"Is it? Thank you, honey," he said looking at me smugly while leaning towards Jules for a kiss. She turned her head offering him her cheek. And while he kissed her, her eyes flicked over at me. After throwing herself at him when she arrived, it was like her feelings had changed. Was I the cause of that? I knew that was just wishful thinking, but maybe.

"You see, Reed, it is amazing. If you have to do island life, this is how you do it. Now, let's go check out my new estate," Laine said insufferably.

As we approached the dock, Laine abandoned Jules for the bow of the boat. It looked like he was going to be the one to stand on the dock and rope us off, but of course he didn't. When he was close enough, he crossed onto the dock and just kept walking. He left all of us behind. I was about to help Monty dock us when he showed that he didn't need either of our help. So, instead, I looked over at Jules allowing her eyes to meet mine.

With us both staring at each other, I wondered what I was supposed to do. Standing in front of me was Jules, the woman I had thought about for so long. It was like I was again the tongue-tied college guy. Was this who I was destined to be whenever I was around her?

I was almost sure that it was until, without even thinking about it, I lifted my hand offering to her. It was to help her cross the slightly rolling boat. She took it and smiled.

Feeling her fingers on mine sent a pulse of electricity through me. Had I ever touched her before? I didn't think I had. But here I was.

My heart was racing. Her delicate fingers lightly gripped mine. I never wanted her to let go. And, knowing what I had to do next, I led her across the boat and helped her onto the dock.

As she stepped onto the wooden planks, I loosened my grip. Accepting that the stolen moment was over, I was expecting my hand to slip from hers. For a second it didn't. For a second, she tightened her grip as if she wasn't ready to let go of me. Wait, did that just happen or was it just in my head?

My hand was away from hers before I could tell. She was still staring at me, though. And with her unspoken words and lingering smile, she seemed to be saying something to me which I couldn't interpret. If I had to guess, it would be that she wanted me too. Obviously, that wasn't it. But, what else could it mean?

"Yep, this is the way you do island life," Laine repeated from ahead of us.

Hearing his words, the moment between Jules and me quickly slipped away. That made me resent Laine even more. The man had everything, money, looks, …he had an island estate for Christ's sake. He definitely didn't deserve Jules too.

"What do you think? We could settle in and then head out to do some fishing?" Laine suggested.

"Since when do you fish?" I challenged wearing thin of his pompousness. "Do you even know how to bait a hook? By the way, when it's baited, the hook part goes in there," I said pointing to the water.

Jules laughed. I didn't expect her too. It felt good. Laine heard her and looked back. Clearly, he didn't like it because it got him to stop, wait for her to reach him, and then put his arm around her. It pissed me off that he was staking claim to her. I tried to see how Jules felt about it, but she was facing the other direction.

"Ha ha," he said sarcastically. "What? You thought I was going to be sticking worms on hooks? What do you think I brought you along for?" he said with a smirk.

"You really think of me as the help, don't you?" I said having had enough.

"There are two types in this world, Reed. Those who do things, and those who help. I think it's good to know which one we are," he said with another smug smile.

"Fuck you, Laine," I said loud enough for him to hear, but not loud enough to make a scene.

"Laine!" I heard Jules chastise as I walked away.

"What? Ask him. He likes to help," Laine said justifying his asshole comment to the woman who agreed to marry him. "Reed, don't you like to help?"

I ignored him and continued towards the house. When I was a little more than halfway there, Laine, Jules and the golf cart passed me. Watching the two of them enter the house, I eventually followed in behind them scanning the space for the kitchen.

Laine hadn't waited for me as he explored his new house, which was good. I was no longer in the mood. What I needed was a drink. Crossing the elegantly decorated foyer and living room, that was where I headed.

"Hi," I said to the portly woman making dinner.

"Good evening, sir," she said pleasantly.

"I'm not a sir. You can save that for the owner of this place. I'll apologize for him now, by the way. I'm Reed."

"Evening," she said awkwardly.

"Listen, where can I find a drink?"

"Beers are in the fridge. The bar is in the living room. It's back where you came from."

"A beer is fine," I said opening the fridge.

Grabbing two of the local beers I opened both of them. Immediately knocking back the first one, I found the garbage and began to sip the second. Feeling the warmth wash through me, I closed my eyes and enjoyed the feeling. I was going to need a lot of these to make it through this trip. And when I finally felt calm enough to continue, I opened my eyes. The portly woman was staring at me with her mouth open.

"You're gonna need a raise," I told her before exiting the kitchen and exploring the rest of the house.

I had to admit, this was a really nice house. The floors were dark wood which I had never seen in the Bahamas. It would make sense that I wouldn't have. The humidity was often 98% and wooden floors were known to warp.

Scattered around the floor were thick, handwoven rugs. On side tables were hand carven wooden statues. And on the walls were the finest example of island art that I had ever seen.

Laine was right. This was the way to do island life if you could afford it. This was way beyond my pay scale, however. Hell, a moderately priced dinner was usually beyond my pay scale. A place like this was pretty much beyond my fantasies.

After checking out the first floor, I next exited the far sliding glass door and took in the back yard. Blooming fruit trees dominated a football field-sized lawn. It really was an estate. This place had to cost Laine a fortune.

Maybe Laine was right about his assessment of me. Maybe I had made a mistake retreating here after college. Why had I been so quick to escape life after graduation?

With the alcohol slowly filling my system, I could admit that Jules wasn't the only reason why. There were a few more things I was dealing with back then that weren't helped by having a conservative judge as a father. I should have asked Jules out, but I never had. As strongly as I had felt for her, I didn't want to lie to her. And, back then, that's what asking her out felt like because there was shit that I had yet to deal with.

It was with that thought and my alcohol-induced lowered inhibitions that I returned to the house ready for whatever would come next. Pulling open the sliding glass door, I entered the family room. Passing through the hall I was surprised to find Jules standing by herself in front of a window in the living room. Hearing me she turned around.

"You have to see this view," she said excitedly calling me over.

Feeling very relaxed, I crossed the room and approached her. I didn't stop until my chest was an inch from her shoulder blade. I could feel her body heat on me. I could smell her.

Turning and finding me there, she paused. Perhaps I should have backed away giving her space. I didn't want to. I wanted her to feel me next to her. She did. When she continued talking, her slowed speech reflected my heated presence.

"You can see the ocean from here," she said as her shoulder softly touched my chest.

"Yeah, it's beautiful," I said only looking at her.

Taking deeper breaths, she looked down at my hand. "What's that?"

I lifted the bottle I was holding and looked at it. "It's a local beer," I said offering her a taste while giving her the space to turn.

"Can I?" she asked allowing our fingers to touch as she took the bottle.

Enjoying the sensation, I extended the moment before releasing it to her. She looked into my eyes as she lifted the bottle to her lips. Slowly letting the chilled, golden drink glide through her warm body, she lowered the bottle and touched her lips. The longer she held the pose, the more I thought about kissing her. The heat between us was overwhelming. And just as I leaned in, Laine's voice echoed down the enclosed stairs.

"Did you find Reed?"

Jules and I tore away from the energy which had bound us together. Breaking our connection hurt. My heart throbbed as it readjusted to its loneliness. And, not able to look up at her in fear that I would never be able to look away, I averted my eyes and headed for the kitchen.

"That one's almost empty. Did you want another?" I asked still not looking up.

"Please," she said reminding me how much I wanted to hold her.

"Bring me one of those, too," Laine requested in an obliviously, cheerful tone.

Reentering the kitchen I had to wonder what had just happened between Jules and me. There was no way she didn't know what she was doing. She had to feel about me the way I felt about her. That was the only explanation.

Had she always felt that way? Had she felt this way in college? She was now engaged, though. What would she be willing to do about it now?

"I'm sorry, I didn't get your name," I said to the portly chef.

"Mildred," she said pleasantly.

"So, how are you today, Mildred?" I asked delaying my eventual return to the happy couple.

"I good, ya know," she said in a sing-song accent. "That's good."

"Can I help ya find someting?"

"No, I'm good. I really think I am," I said answering a question she didn't ask.

Retrieving three more beers, I opened them and headed back into the living room. Jules and my eyes immediately met. Quickly looking at Laine, I gave him a polite smile and handed him a beer.

"I'm glad to see you've finally relaxed," Laine told me as he took a swig.

I looked Jules in the eyes as I handed her the second bottle. "I really have," I said washed in warmth as she held my gaze.

"Good. I was beginning to believe that you were going to be a stick in the mud this whole trip."

"Nope, I just needed to check out the amazing view," I said still staring at Jules.

"Nice." Laine held out his bottle. "Then, how about we cheers to a memorable trip?"

"I'll cheers to that," I told him touching my bottle with his.

"To a memorable trip," Jules added joining in.

For the next hour, I allowed Laine to show off the website-supplied details of his new home. Passing from room to room, each seemed like a revelation to Laine. It had been a lot of years since I had seen Laine this happy.

For the life of me, I couldn't figure out why he was. Didn't he already have homes in Calabasas and New York? What was another home to him?

He really did seem to want me to be excited for him, though, so I did what I could to play along. When he bragged about the brand of the couch, I nodded as if I was impressed. And when we walked his estate picking fruit, I told him how big of a deal the selection was.

Frankly, though, I couldn't give a shit. The only thing he had that meant anything to me was walking on the other side of him, and I was going to do anything I had to to make her mine.

By the time we sat for dinner, I had already had five beers. There wasn't much that was going to bother me at that point. The woman I had spent a lifetime in love with was seated across from me and she was looking at me like I had always dreamed about.

I didn't know where any of this was going, but I knew where I wanted it to go. I wanted it to go to my bedroom. For years I had imagined what I would do to her if I had gotten the chance. Now, there she was undressing me with her eyes. It was a really great day.

With the household staff gone after dinner, Jules and I cleared the table. I kept expecting her to steal a moment with me once we were alone in the kitchen. It never happened. She never even looked at me. She was blushing the entire time, though. I felt like I was in her head. I liked being in her head. It was a good start.

"Why don't we have a drink on the veranda?" Laine suggested to the three of us.

"Here they call it a patio," I had to tell him.

"When you pay this much for a place, it's called a veranda," Laine said in an almost self-deprecating way.

I chuckled. Laine looked at me and smiled.

"You two go ahead. It's been a long day from me. I think I'm gonna head up," Jules said barely drawing Laine's attention.

"Okay," her fiancé said.

"You sure? You should join us. We never really got the chance to catch up," I said disappointed.

"No. I'm tired. But, you two have fun."

"Okay," her loving fiancé said again.

Wishing her a good night, Laine and I grabbed stiffer drinks and got comfortable on the patio furniture. I had to admit, for patio furniture, it was nice.

"So, what do you think?" Laine asked.

"Of Jules? She's nice."

"Not of her. What do you think of the place?"

It was so like Laine to not give a shit about the woman he was with. I decided to let it slide.

"It's nice. I'm sure it's worth whatever you paid for it."

"I don't know about that. This place set me back. They didn't want to sell. But, it was the best of the best, so I figured I had to get it."

"How very you of you," I said unable to imagine anything that would be more like him.

"I didn't just get his place for me, though. You know that, right?"

"Who did you get it for, you and Jules?" I said truly not giving a shit anymore.

"No. I got it for you and me. And mostly for you," he said clearly drunker than I was.

"For me? How did you get this for me?"

"I mean, it's not like I'm ever down here. You live here. If I'm not using it, someone may as well."

What he said didn't register because nothing that he was saying was making sense. Like I said, he was clearly drunker than I was and I truly didn't give a shit.

"Well, Laine, I don't know if you realize this, but I have a home. I know that the whole thing could probably fit on your veranda, but it's mine. And, what's more, it's where my family is."

"What are you talking about? Your family lives in Chicago."

"Yeah, that's what you never got in all the times you visited. The people on that island are my family. They're the family I chose. So, why would I want to be alone here when I instead could be back there surrounded by people who care about me?"

That pretty much shut Laine up, and thank god. There would be no use explaining things like family and love to him. The only thing he ever cared about anymore was himself and his possessions. He would sell a child into slavery if it meant he could upgrade to the leather package in his next sports car. I wasn't sure why I had put up with him for so long.

"I think I'm gonna head to bed, too," I eventually told him after sitting quietly in the moonlight.

"Yeah. I think I'll stick around here for a while."

"You do that. Good night," I said before knocking back the last of my drink and heading upstairs to my assigned room.

I'm not gonna lie, while walking to my room it took some effort to prevent things from spinning. Behind my closed door, I pulled off my shirt allowing it to drop to the floor beside me. I had just unbuttoned and unzipped my pants when my door suddenly flew open. Before I could react, someone had entered and closed the door behind them. It was Jules, and dressed in the sheerest of nightdresses, she was irresistible.

"I…" she began before I crossed the room, grabbed the back of her neck, and kissed her hard.

Feeling her lips against mine sent a pulse through my body unlike anything I had ever felt. I was lost to the sensation. It was 14 years in the building and the sudden release of it rocked me to my core.

More aroused than I had ever been, I dropped my hand to her ass and pulled her towards me. She responded by wrapping her arms around my chest and her legs around my hips. Cradling her body on mine, I carried her to the bed. Still locked in an embrace, I crawled onto the mattress and placed her on her back. Released from her grip, I moved from between her legs and tore off my pants.

Panting naked in front of the woman I had loved for so long, I was an animal about to pounce. Her thighs rubbed together in feverish anticipation. Her barely covered breasts heaved. She wanted me as much as I wanted her. And, with nothing left to stop us, I threw my body on top of hers removing her panties as soon as I did.

My throbbing cock touched her pulsing pussy and sparks flew. It electrified me. I wanted to savor the moment but I ached for her. Every second that I wasn't inside of her tore my soul apart. So when I aligned my head with her dripping opening and pushed, I curled my back as if able to take the first unhindered breath of my life.

Gripping my cock, Jules's pussy was steaming hot. She consumed me. Quivering beneath me, she reached up and dug her nails into my back. Raking them across, she removed strips of skin. It added to my pleasure. And when I pulled back my hips to plunge in again, her face froze beginning her unrelenting clench.

Thrusting harder and harder, my groin slammed against her body. Holding back, she squeaked as she did. Their melodic pitches were getting higher. And when she yelped beyond what I could hear, I exploded inside of her twitching wildly as I did.

Once I started cumming I couldn't stop. And once my thrusts relented, Jules let go of her pent up pleasure and came. The moment was everything I ever hoped it would be. I never wanted it to end. I wanted to hold her in my arms forever. And if I had had anything to say about it, that would have been what would have happened next.

Chapter 3

Laine

Well, this was not working out as I had planned. How the hell did I get here? You know what? This is all because of Reed. Fuckin' Reed. What does that guy have over me?

From the moment I saw him during our first week of college, he's been all I can think about. Not every moment of every day, of course. I'm not a psychopath. Just enough that there has got to be something wrong with me.

Since the beginning, the man had a vulnerability about him. Basically the first time we spent any time alone, he admitted to me that he was a virgin. Who does that? After that, he told me about his insecurities and then his father. He was like an open book. I couldn't help but wanna take care of him.

I spent the next four years doing nothing but trying to get him laid and catering to his every whim. I had forgotten about the polka-dots story. But yeah, I did that too. For some reason, he had gotten it into his head that he wouldn't walk without putting florescent pink polka-dots on his graduation gown. Who thinks that?

So, what did I have to do? I had to go around asking everyone on our floor for a stapler, check all of the computer rooms, and then finally start breaking into supply closets. Somewhere there's probably video surveillance footage of me committing a felony and it is all because he couldn't graduate without his polka-dots.

To be honest, I probably went into investment banking because of him. He was this incredibly good looking kid from a rich family. His father was a judge for Christ's sake. What did my father do? He ran out on me and my mom. I like to say that my father was a runner, but now you know what I mean by it.

I spent my teens with nothing. My mother could barely pay the rent. We were dirt poor. My high school friends weren't rich, but at least they had heat in the winter. We had a house full of donated blankets.

How was I supposed to take care of a rich kid like Reed coming from where I had? I couldn't. So, I went into the most lucrative business I could think of, investment banking, and I killed it.

While everyone else was going broke during the recession, I was making my first million. A week later I made my first ten million. I am a god damn self-made man.

I came from absolutely nothing, made myself rich, and didn't blow it all once I did. I now have enough money to last me five lifetimes and all Reed does is make me feel like shit for it. Why do I even put up with him?

It's because I can't quit him, that's why. I've tried. Believe me, I have god damn tried. But I can't get him out of my head. Do you know how many women I've fucked trying to wash him out of my mind? The cum spilled would drown us all.

But yet, nothing. The thought of him keeps coming back. 50 weeks of the year I spend vowing that I won't visit him. Then, I always do, and like clockwork, he spends our week together making me feel horrible for my making something of my life.

At the same time, he's thrown his life away. He lives in a fuckin' shack. I've been to the home he grew up in. His current place could fit in his childhood bedroom. Which raises the question, how much money does a judge make?

I once asked him if his father was on the take. Let me tell you, he did not like that! But I know what things cost. An honest judge couldn't afford a place like where he grew up. Things didn't add up.

Anyway, he goes from living in a place like that needing nothing, to a place like his shack needing everything. The man doesn't have a TV. I once offered to buy him one and he replied, "What am I gonna do with that?"

You watch it, you freak! What's wrong with him?

And then I buy him this home. The thing cost me 20 million dollars. Do you think I give a shit about having a house on an island in the middle of nowhere? Let me assure you, I do not. But he likes being in the middle of nowhere. Fine! Be in the middle of nowhere. But live there in style.

And, what was that crap he said about family? Those people on that island aren't his family. I'm more his family than they are. I was there every day for him when he was a lonely, scared, freshman. He was a virgin and I got him laid. I sat and listened to him go on for hours about Jules. For fucking HOURS! Do you think I liked that shit? No! But I did it because that was what he needed and all I wanted to do was take care of him.

I even thought that if I found Jules and I could convince her to pretend to love me, he would see how much he has misjudged me. If I could get the girl he always wanted and could never get, didn't that mean that I was good enough for him? Yeah, it would. It would make me a god damn legend.

Has it, though? I don't see any difference. In fact, he's kind of being more of a dick. What was up with him telling that Thanksgiving story? What was the point of that?

Yeah, I grew up dirt poor while his father was a judge. We get it, you were better than I was. But who's the rich son-of-a-bitch now? That's right, me. So why doesn't he show me some god damn respect? I just can't friggin' win with him.

Sitting on my veranda weighing all of this, I realized that my glass was now empty. Making a move to get up to get another one, I wobbled. Recalling the number of drinks I had, I lost count at six. That's when I decided that it might be better for me to head to bed.

Peeling myself off of the couch, I stumbled towards the stairs. Climbing them, I consider stopping by Reed's room to tell him about his ungrateful ass. But, not even I was drunk enough for that.

Instead, I worked my way down the upstairs hall to the master bedroom and entered expecting to see Jules there. She wasn't. That was kind of a problem because we never decided on a sleeping arrangement.

I looked over at the ensuite bathroom door. It was open and the lights were off. Well, wherever she was, she just lost the right to dictate where I slept.

Heading to the bed, I pulled off my shirt and clumsily rid myself of my pants. While doing that, I might have gotten my foot caught and I might have almost face-planted the ground. Might have! But if no one saw it, did it actually happen?

Crawling into what, at that moment, felt like the most comfortable bed I had ever been in, I pulled up the covers. About to bring this sucky day to an end, the bedroom door opened. Jules walked in. She was wearing a sheer nightgown which barely covered her ass or hid her nipples. What the hell was this?

You know, I did feel chemistry between us the day we met. And I always did love the thicker girls. If this night ended in sex, it would make up for so much.

"Hey there," I said pouring on the charm.

"I just had sex with Reed."

Ahh shit! Nope, that sounded about right. Because so far, this little venture of mine has turned into a complete cluster fuck. So, why wouldn't the guy I'm trying to impress have sex with my fiancé?

"I'm so sorry. I didn't mean for it to happen. It just did," she explained looking guilty and justifiably worried.

"You fucked Reed?"

"Well, that isn't the word I would use, but I guess that would accurately describe what we did. Yeah. What does this mean?" She asked concerned yet still not covering her nips.

Were her nipples supposed to be distracting me? If so, it wasn't working… I mean, for the most part it wasn't working. Looking at them did calm me a little, but they didn't stop me from feeling fucking pissed.

"I think we should tell him that we're not really engaged."

"You didn't tell him?" I asked her suddenly seeing an opening.

"No. I didn't want to break our deal."

"But you thought that fucking the guy who our fake relationship was supposed to impress, didn't?"

"Sometimes fiancés cheat?" She said offering the worst possible excuse.

As I let Jules and her freed nipples sweat, I allowed this new information to float around in my alcohol-soaked brain. Maybe I could use this. Yeah, it's fucking humiliating. At least it would be if Jules were really my fiancé. But, she isn't. It sucks that Reed thought he could do this to me, but doesn't this bring Mr. High and Mighty down a peg?

He keeps talking about how much of an asshole I am, but he just slept with the fiancé of his oldest friend. What type of dick does that? I think I have him.

"Laine, I feel awful about what I did. I really think we should tell him the truth," Jules pleaded giving me more leverage over her with every word.

"Are you saying that you no longer need the money?"

"No, I completely need the money. You don't know how much I need the money."

Yeah, keep talking.

"Then why did you do it?"

"I don't know. It's been a while for me, I guess? I didn't expect to see him and it might have stirred up some feelings?"

"But, you need the money?"

"I definitely need the money."

"Then, you're not going to tell him."

"You sure? Because if we tell him…"

"You're not gonna tell him," I demanded cutting her off. "And, you're not gonna fuck him again."

"I got it. That will definitely not happen again. I'm so sorry it happened this time. And you can rest assured that it was for the first and last time."

"Good," I said deciding that I couldn't have planned it better if I had tried. Not only has this become something I could hold over his righteous head, but it gave me an exit strategy for this investment. If I told Reed that I ended it with Jules because I found out she cheated on me, he would never question the legitimacy of it all.

Ya know, as bad as the day had gone, it might have just taken an upswing.

"So, umm, where should I sleep?" she asked realizing she was no longer the one with the control. "I guess I should take the floor?"

"Maybe that's for the best," I said enjoying what was going on.

I watched as Jules grabbed a pillow and tossed it onto the floor. It almost made me feel good watching her squirm. Almost.

"No. Stop. I'm not going to let you sleep on the floor. You can have the bed. I'll sleep on the floor," I said clearly stupidly drunk.

"I can't let you sleep on the floor," she insisted.

"Why not?"

"Because I'm the one who screwed up. If anyone's gonna sleep on the floor, it's me."

"I already told you, you don't have to sleep on the floor."

"And neither do you," she said hinting at another option.

"Then how about if we both just take the bed."

"You'll be okay with that?" She asked me letting me know that she really did feel bad about what she did.

"Yeah. I'm fine with it. You don't snore, do you?"

"Maybe a little," she said to my surprise. Who admitted something like that?

"Okay fine. But if you start rattling the windows, I'm turning you over."

"Deal," she said with the beginnings of a smile.

I could see why Reed liked her so much. The honesty, the vulnerability, the nips... Back in college, I never got it. But, I could kinda see it now.

Watching her climb into bed next to me, I took a moment to picture the two of them having sex. If it wasn't for all of the betrayal, the image would have been hot. There had to be a part of Reed that was beside himself with joy. He finally got to fuck the famous Jules. There was a part of me that was actually happy for him. There was another part of me that wanted to make him squirm like the worm he was. But for tonight, I was going to let the happy part win out.

"Night," Jules told me once she was comfortably tucked in beside me.

"Night, Jules," I told her seeing her in a different light… literally a different light. The nightstand lamps were casting amazing looking shadows on her. She kind of looked like an angel.

Anyway, my intention for the next few hours was to come up with a plan. Knowing what I had to do, I turned off the light, leaned back, pictured tomorrow and… zzzzz.

When I woke up the next morning, my first thought was that I wasn't hungover. It took me a minute to realize that it was because I was still drunk. How much did I drink?

Opening my eyes, another more pressing question came to mind. What was it that Reed told me last night that got me so upset, and what did Jules say that made me feel better? It took a few more minutes for everything to come rushing back. I had told Reed that he could live on the private island, and he had thrown it back in my face. How could I have forgotten that?

What a dick move. Do you think he could have at least have been appreciative? I basically gave him a 20 million dollar private island. Didn't that deserve a thank you? Thank you, Laine, for giving me a place to live that's bigger than a garage. Thank you, Laine, for thinking of me even though I constantly treat you like trash.

Nope. Nothing. But, starting today, things were gonna be different. I could barely wait to see him again to watch his I'm-all-about-what's-moral ass squirm.

Thinking about it, I almost jumped out of bed. When I say almost, I'm not talking about jumping. I definitely jumped. It's the "out of bed" part that I didn't make. And having moved a solid foot towards the edge, I reconsider my enthusiasm and again got comfortable.

"Are you okay?" I heard someone say behind me.

Deciding that my attempt really did happen, I groaned positive that I could make words come out. Nope. Apparently not.

"I can't tell, are you still sleeping?"

She asked me another question. What was with all of the questions? What was this, an interrogation?

"I'm awake," I forced my lips to say.

"Oh. I was waiting for you to wake up to ask how you wanted to go down."

"Using the stairs?" I suggested thinking it should have been obvious.

"No. I mean, did you want to go down together? Did you want me to act guilty around him, or like I was sneaking around?"

For this, I lifted my head and looked at her. The woman definitely had a devious side. Her impulse to come up with a detailed plan was amazing.

"I don't know. How did you leave things with him?"

"I pretty much said that we had made a mistake. He asked me if I truly loved you, and I told him that I had to go."

That sneaky bastard. He was trying to snake me out of my fiancé.

"I know we talked about it last night, but are you sure we shouldn't tell him?"

"Yes," I insisted.

"Okay. Just checking," she said looking away disappointedly.

What was up with her? Was she really that horny? If so, I might have a cure for that.

"We're gonna go downstairs together. You're gonna act like you made the biggest mistake of your life. As soon as you're alone with him, you're going to tell him that what happened will never happen again. And that I am the greatest lover you have ever had in your life, and that he doesn't even compare."

"I'm not gonna say that?" Jules said shocked.

"Is it the greatest lover part?"

"Yes!"

"Okay. I was just testing. But tell him that it will never happen again. Oh, and remind him that I'm incredibly hung."

"Why would I remind him of that? How would that even come up in conversation?"

"I don't know. You can say that after giving it some thought you decided that you can't leave me because, on top of all of my other wonderful qualities, I'm also incredibly hung."

"I don't know if I could say that honestly."

"What do you mean?"

"I mean that I don't want to belabor the point, but Reed was pretty big. He was legit big."

Staring at Jules I wondered what I should say next. The interesting thing was that after saying that, she paused. Not only did she pause, but her eyes flicked down towards my sheet covered dick. After returning her gaze to my eyes, her eyes flicked down again.

Wait, was she trying to get me to prove it?

Not sure what I should do, I stared intently at her watching her every move. After returning to my eyes, her eyes flick down for the third time. Yeah, she was trying to get me to prove it. Oh, bring it on!

I moved my hand and grabbed the edge of the sheet giving her one last chance to back down. When that didn't happen, I pulled back the cover. It was morning so I was fully hard. Reed and I had skinny-dipped together so I had seen his junk. He was big, but…

"I'm still not saying it," Jules conceded while being very slow to look away.

When she eventually did I replaced the sheet. I had to admit, that was kind of fun. Who was this still half-naked woman lying beside me? Except for my opposition research, I barely knew anything about her.

That was a query for another day, though. Right now we had to lock down our plan.

"Fine. But be sure to act like you feel guilty. And make sure you tell him that it will never happen again."

"That should be easy because I do feel guilty and it won't happen again."

"Good. Now I guess I should get up so that we can head down together."

"If that's what you wanna do," she said sitting up as if waiting for the show to begin.

Never wanting to disappoint the fans, I pulled back the sheet sure to give her another good view. She lapped it up. She didn't even pretend to be looking anywhere else. And I was hard. I mean, really hard. What can I say? The big guy likes a show.

Heading to the bathroom giving her a full view of my ass, I looked back to make sure she was still watching. She was. In spite of a few missteps, I was really starting to like her. I was almost disappointed when I finally entered the bathroom. And, the only reason I say 'almost' was because I had to pee like a racehorse.

Heading downstairs with Jules in tow, my eyes bounced around looking for Reed. I couldn't wait to see the look on his face. It had been so long since I was the morally superior one. What would it even feel like?

Not finding him in the living room, I led Jules to the kitchen. I found Reed sitting at the marble island drinking coffee. Now, that dude was hungover.

"Hey Reed, how'd you sleep?" I asked cheerily and a little loud.

"Fine," he replied not looking up.

"Fine? Good. I'm glad you slept well. There's no reason not to sleep well here. There's no stress. Just me, your oldest friend and the woman I love, truly love. After a lifetime of searching, the woman I absolutely love," I said watching him like a hawk.

He lifted his head and looked at me. Instead of wilting, his eyes sharpened. "Yeah, I couldn't have slept better."

"That's good. There's no reason why you wouldn't have the best sleep of your life, right?"

Not giving an inch, "Nope, no reason in the world."

"Good."

"Yep, good," he said now staring me down.

That duplicitous bastard.

"I'm making some souse," the thick, dark-skinned woman said from across the kitchen.

"Huh?" I said shifting my gaze.

Reed interrupted. "Mildred is saying that she made souse for breakfast."

"What's souse," Jules said moving to my side.

"It's like a soup." Reed turned to the woman. "Pig's feet?"

"Chicken."

"Yeah, chicken souse. It's a Bahamian thing. It's served with grits and a biscuit. It's good. Thanks, Mildred."

"You're welcome, sir."

"I told you, call me Reed," he said forcing a smile in her direction.

She smiled back but didn't reply.

"Well, that sounds delightful," I said not giving a shit about anything he had just said. "Listen, I thought we'd do some fishing today."

"If that's what you want," Reed confirmed. "Laine Toros always gets what he wants."

"So nice of you to realize that," I said playing along.

"It's hard to miss," Reed said before allowing his eyes to bounce across to Jules.

I wasn't sure what that look meant but it meant something. It was as good of a time as any for Jules to drop the bomb.

"Mildred, have you seen the boat driver?"

"You mean Monty?" Reed corrected… like a dick.

"Yeah, Mildred, have you seen him?"

"He probably at the dock. He mostly stays down d'ear."

"Great. And, I can't wait for some of that incredible sounding chicken souse," I told her reminding Reed which of us was the charming one.

Heading down to the dry dock, I found Monty lounging in a chair listening to the news on the radio. Seeing me enter, he got up.

"I was thinking we could do some fishing today," I told him.

"You want the big game stuff or the regular stuff?"

"What's the difference?"

"We could go deep water fishing for marlins or sharks. They about 100, 200 pounds. Or, we could go for snappers and groupers. They still get big but dey ain't dat big."

"Why don't you surprise us," I said with a smile.

"You got it, sir."

"Excellent. Maybe in two hours."

"I'll be here."

I turned to go and then he said, "Sir, what did you want to do about tomorrow?"

"What do you mean?"

"It's Sunday. It's the lord's day."

"I'm not going to church if that's what you're asking."

"No. It's the staff's day off. I was wonderin' if you were gunna need me."

"So, no one's gonna be here?"

"Mildred will make sure you have plenty to eat."

"Oh, I was wondering."

Monty laughed. "No, she'll set you up good. I was wonderin' if you would need me?"

"No. Have your day off. The boat will be here, though, right?"

"Yes, sir. Do you know how to drive it?"

"I've driven high-performance sports cars. It's a boat in open water. I think I can figure it out," I said a little snippy from the suggestion.

"Then you'll probably get it. Just don't get yourself lost," he said with a chuckle.

I had to admit, that was a good point. "I'll stick around here."

Monty nodded with a smile.

When I got back to the house, the mood between Jules and Reed was noticeably different. Jules gave me a look telling me she had done it. Reed's self-righteous ass could no longer look me in the eyes. Now we were getting somewhere.

"Bring on that souse!" I said before happily planting my ass next to my betraying best friend.

My two travel mates were pretty quiet for the next few hours. Jules spoke when I engaged her in conversation, but she made no effort to keep the conversation going. It made fishing a peaceful experience. And things got exciting when Reed reeled in a twenty-pound turbot. It really fought, which made me wonder how much a hundred pounder would fight back.

"Look at you! I didn't know you knew how to do this," I told Reed.

"It isn't my first fishing trip," he said loosening up.

"You get out often?"

"Couple times a year."

"Well, the house will be here. Feel free to take the boat out anytime."

"Thanks. Maybe," Reed said finally starting to understand the extent of my offer.

After a few more hours and beers, we headed back to the house to rest up for dinner. As we did, I made note of how Monty handled the boat. It all seemed pretty simple. There was a steering wheel and a throttle with forward and reverse. Any idiot could drive a boat. I didn't see what the big deal was.

Back on land, the conversation turned to Jules. That was Reed's doing.

"What do think? Do you think you could live this life?" he asked.

"You mean, having breakfast served to me and then spending the day fishing? I think I could probably suffer through it."

"What about if you didn't have a chef and private island?" Reed continued.

"I don't know. It would take some getting used to. It's not like I have a life in Calabasas. Most of the time it's just me hanging out with my mother."

"You mean until this one started jet-setting you around?" Reed said pointing at me.

"Oh, yeah. No, yeah it's completely different now. Paris... where else? The Bahamas. No, it's wild," she said before latching her arm around mine and allowing the conversation to die.

I had to admit, seeing the look on his face as Jules held onto me was worth the $200,000 I was paying her. It was clearly eating him up. There was a small part of me that felt bad for him, but come on, he deserved this.

For 14 years I had been nothing but loyal to him. I had considered not forgiving him for sleeping with Jules, but who was I kidding? I could never stay mad at him. And, believe me, I've tried.

After washing up, we all sat down for a drink before being served dinner. I had to admit, the chef was very good. Grouper fingers, peas n' rice, macaroni and cheese, it was all very filling but good. Then for dessert, we had something called guava duff. It was this cake/pudding thing with slices of a fruit called guava in it. Poured over it was a white sauce that tasted like sugar and rum. It had to be the best dessert I'd ever had.

"If there's nothing else, I'll head out," Mildred said.

"No. We're good here. You can head out."

"There's plenty left for tomorrow. But I also made a pot of peas soup and dumplings. It's in the fridge. You just have to put it on the stove to warm it up."

"Thank you. It sounds delightful," I said making sure Reed knew how gracious I could be. "Have a good weekend."

After sitting around the table for a while, we moved to the veranda. Jules joined us this time and I took the opportunity to get to know her a little better.

"What was the first thing you did after graduation?" I asked her.

"You mean after packing up my stuff?"

"Yeah."

"I flew home with my mom."

"When did you move to Seattle?" Reed asked.

"A few months later. I had a friend who was from there and she invited me up to live with her."

"Do you like it up there?" Reed continued.

"It's changed a lot over the last few years. The tech bubble really reshaped things."

"You mean because of Amazon?" I asked.

"Yeah, them. But others as well. Lots of awkward tech nerds live there now. Lots of meth. The culture of the city has changed a lot."

"Lots of meth? Damn! I wouldn't have guessed that," I said.

"Yeah, you have to be there to see it. They don't exactly put that on the brochures."

"I don't see why not," I said. "Come for the tech. Stay for the meth. The commercial writes itself."

Both Reed and Jules laughed.

"What about you two? What were the first things you did after college?"

"It was actually the same things," Reed explained.

"Yeah. I headed to his place staying there for a week. I got to experience the judge up close. He's quite the guy."

"My father is quite the guy," Reed echoed before taking a swig.

"How did you end up in New York?" Jules asked me.

"It was the judge. He put me in contact with one of his friends who offered me a job. Without him, I wouldn't be the man I am today."

"Then I guess it's my turn to apologize to you," Reed told me reminding me that I had said the same to him. I'll admit that it stung a little.

"By the way, you know why he did that, right?" Reed continued.

"I don't know. Helping out his son's friend?"

"No. He didn't do anything out of the goodness of his heart. He just did it because he wanted to get you as far away from me as possible."

If it was Reed's goal to get under my skin, that had worked. "Why would he want to separate us?"

"Because he's a conservative prick. He didn't like how close we were. He thought you were a bad influence on me."

"How was I a bad influence on you?"

"I don't know. By looking out for me. Basically, my father thought I was gay and that you were my boyfriend. So, he wanted to get you as far away from me as possible."

"He thought I was your boyfriend?" I asked with a laugh that masked how uncomfortable I suddenly was. "Why would he think that?"

"I mean, we did spend a lot of time together back then. There was a stretch there when we literally spent every night together."

"Junior year," I reminded him.

"Yeah. That's right," he said surprised that I would remember.

"You were obsessed with…" I caught myself before I said it.

"What?" Jules asked. "What were you obsessed with?"

"You," Reed replied. "I was so in love with you. At least, I thought I was. Every night he and I would eat dinner and I would go on and on about you and about how beautiful you were and how much I liked you. I'm sure it drove Laine insane," Reed said with a nostalgic chuckle. "But, to his credit, he listened. And now look at you two, the perfect pair."

Well, that certainly put a damper on the conversation.

"I think I'll head up to bed. I didn't get much sleep last night and it was a long day," Reed said.

"Us too," I told him patting Jules on the thigh.

Following Reed upstairs we headed in opposite directions and then said good night. Behind the closed door, Jules broke her silence.

"Did you all really talk about me every night your junior year?"

"I'm sure it wasn't every night. But, yeah, your name came up a lot."

"Huh," she said suddenly lost in thought.

I stripped down to my boxer briefs and watched as Jules changed into her sheer nightdress. Not only was she not wearing a bra, but she wasn't shy about it. She had to be doing this for my benefit. I didn't forget about how she had been checking me out this morning. She was definitely into me. And, all that talk about college had seemed to put her into a mood. The night was definitely about to get interesting.

Jules was about to join me in bed when she said, "I'm gonna go grab some water. Did you want any?"

"Sure," I said knowing that this wasn't the time to refuse anything she offered.

"Okay," she said leaving the bedroom and closing the door behind her.

I had about two minutes to do anything I had to do to prepare. Jumping out of bed, I sprinted to the bathroom. Sniffing my pits and checking my breath, I quickly gargle. After, I gave myself a small squirt of cologne, put a few condoms in the nightstand drawer, and scurried back into bed.

Making a last-minute decision, I whipped off my underwear and tossed them aside. Feeling comfortable and prepared, I then leaned back and waited for Jules to return. It didn't take long and when she returned it was without the water.

"Where's the water?"

"I had sex with Reed again."

Crap!

"When?"

"Just now."

"You were gone for two minutes."

"It didn't take long."

"What's wrong with you?"

"I'm sorry," Jules implored not budging from her spot.

"Seriously, though, what's wrong with you?"

"I can't help it. It was all of that talk about college. I had such a big crush on him back then. So, when I heard how he felt about me…" She shrugged her shoulders and faced her palms towards the ceiling.

I groaned and sunk into the bed.

It was only then that Jules moved to join me on the bed.

"I don't understand why we can't just tell him about us."

"No. If you want to get paid, you won't."

"But you can. Why don't you tell him?" she suggested.

"So, you can fuck him without guilt?"

"I guess "yes" would not be a good answer in this situation?"

"No, it wouldn't."

Jules looked away in thought. "I guess I just don't understand what's supposed to be happening here. You clearly remembered that your best friend had a thing for me. Yet, out of everyone in the world, you brought me with you. Why? Were you trying to make him jealous or something?"

Jules turned to me and read me like a book.

"Wait, you were using me to make him jealous. But why? Why would anyone go through all of that trouble? You're not in love with him, are you?"

"No, why would you say that?" I protested.

"Oh my god, you are! You're in love with him!"

"I'm not in love with him," I insisted.

"You are! You're in love with him. And you brought me to, what, make him jealous? Make him see you in a new light or something?"

"No, that's ridiculous!"

"That's it. You brought me to make him see you in a new light. And then I slept with him. Oh, I'm so sorry. I'm so, so sorry."

Ah, crap!

"I'm not in love with him," I told her resigned. "At least I don't think so."

"But, you are very attracted to him?"

"That would probably be an accurate description."

"For how long?" She asked me.

"I don't know. From the beginning? From the first time I met him."

"Shit."

"Yeah. Shit."

"Does he know?"

"I don't see how he doesn't, but I don't think he does."

"So, all that time listening to him talk about me felt…"

"…like an ice pick repeatedly jammed into my eyeball?"

"Oh my god."

"No, no, I'm exaggerating. It wasn't fun but it wasn't all that. Hell, I was the one who got him laid for the first time. It wasn't that I didn't want him to find someone. It was just that it would have been nice if he could see me the way I saw him."

Jules crawled next to me and cuddled up beside me. Placing her hand on my chest she lightly massaged it. "I'm sorry," she said making me feel like such a pathetic tool.

"So, what do you want to do now?" She asked me stating the million-dollar question.

"I don't know. But you can't tell him I hired you."

"Because it will make you look sad and desperate?"

"Those wouldn't be the words I would use but…"

"I get it. I promise I won't tell him. And, if I had known the situation, I wouldn't have done what I did. I swear."

"I'm sure," I said not believing her. "So, why did you do it? Why did you have sex with him? You said you needed the money. Why would you risk it?"

"I mean, you've seen him, right?"

I sighed. "Yeah, I've seen him."

"He's just so… great."

"Yeah, tell me about it," I said relaxing into Jules's embrace.

"You know, there might be something I could do to help you," Jules offered.

"Why would you do that? Don't you like him too?"

"Yeah, but I don't have your history. If I left here tomorrow there's a chance I might never think about him again… as small as it is. But you, something tells me that you will never stop thinking about him. Like, never, ever."

I groaned and slithered further into the bed. What she said felt uncomfortably true. All I could do was squirm.

"Listen, if you want me to help, I can."

"What could you do?"

"I could put in a good word for you."

"You really think that would help? The man has known me for fourteen years. I really don't think anything you say would make a difference."

"Well, then you tell me. What do you want me to do?"

"Don't do anything. I'll figure this out. Just, stop fucking him."

"I will. I promise."

"You mean, until the next time?"

"No. I only did it because I didn't know. Now I know. I wouldn't do that to you. And, you know, I really need the money. So…"

I chuckled. "Okay. And, since you're being so nice to me, I should probably warn you that I'm naked under here."

Jules looked at me questioningly.

"Yeah, I thought the night was headed in a… ah… different direction."

"I'm just gonna, rollover here," she said leaving my side for the far edge of the bed. "Don't read too much into it. I just… yeah. Good night."

Yep, another perfect ending to another perfect day.

"Good night," I told her before turning off the lights and going to sleep.

The next morning I headed downstairs leaving Jules in the room. Entering the kitchen I found Reed at work in front of the stove. He was warming up breakfast. Who knew that snakes could cook surrounded by all that grass?

"Morning," I told him curious to see his reaction when he saw me.

Reed looked at me and then scanned the room behind me. "Where's Jules?"

"In bed. I think she had something last night that disagreed with her. She must have snuck something when I wasn't looking."

"She probably just saw something she liked and went for it."

"Who knows? That woman would put any piece of garbage in her body."

"I doubt that's it. Maybe I should go up and check on her."

"What are you, a doctor? No, it's probably best if you let her rest. I'll take something up for her later."

"So, she's not gonna join us today?"

"Probably not. But, that will give us a little time to catch up. I feel like I don't know you anymore. What have you been into recently? Anything worth talking about?"

"Nah. You know me. Mr. Predictable."

"Do I know you? Because people change."

"Sometimes it's for the better."

"Sometimes. But, not always," I reminded him.

"You are right about that," he said giving me a lingering stare that made me think he was talking about me. What was that supposed to mean? Yeah, as if I didn't know.

"Do you know something we never talk about?" I asked him.

"What's that?"

"You. Are you dating anyone?"

"Me? No."

"Well, how about before? When was the last time you dated someone?"

"I don't know. It's been a while," he said squirreling away from me.

"When though? When was the last time you dated anyone? I feel like I'm always talking about who I'm dating but you never share."

"Because there's nothing to share."

"Really? No one? Have you even gotten laid since the last time I got you laid?"

"Yeah. Of course."

"Then, who was it? Tell me," I said refusing to let this go.

"I don't know. It was a hookup."

"Someone on the island? One of your family members?" I said with a satisfied smile.

"No. It was a tourist."

"A tourist? Who an American?"

"Yeah. They came down for a fishing trip."

"And what? You ran into them at a bar?"

"No. I was doing some work on the fishing boat and they invited me to get something to eat afterward."

"I see. And, one thing led to another?"

"Yeah."

"And, what, did SHE invite you back to her room?"

"Something like that."

"What does she look like? Big breasts? Is that your type now?"

"Why are you asking me this?"

"I'm just wondering if SHE was everything you hoped she would be? Was that what SHE was? Was she the woman of your dreams?"

Reed stared at me intensely before relenting. "You know."

"Know what?" I asked having started to suspect due to his non-use of pronouns.

"That it was a guy?"

"How would I know that since you didn't tell me?"

"I don't know."

"How long ago was this?"

"About five years."

"Five years ago?" I asked stunned.

"Yeah. Why would it matter?"

"It matters because you never told me."

"Why would I tell you that?"

"Because… I don't know. We're friends."

"Are we?"

"What is that supposed to mean?"

"Why didn't you tell me that you ran into Jules? And don't say that you forgot the way I felt about her because I know you didn't."

"It's because… I knew how you would react."

"If you knew how I would react and we are friends, then maybe you shouldn't have started dating her."

"What? Did you call dibs on her? You get that we aren't college kids anymore, right?"

"I was in love with her for so long? How could that not mean anything to you? Couldn't you consider my feelings for once in your life?"

"*Me* not consider *your* feelings? Oh, that's rich."

"What's that supposed to mean?"

"You know what? Just forget about it."

"No, I wanna know. When have you ever considered my feelings?" Reed asked.

I stared at Reed like he was suffering from amnesia. That had to be it. The only other explanation would be that he was insane.

"You know what? You're right. I have never considered your feelings. You're Mr. Perfect and I'm the devil. Let's just drop it."

"I never said I was perfect."

"No. Of course not. I guess I'm wrong again. Can we drop it now?"

Reed stared at me and then walked away. "You know, you can be a real dick sometimes," he said on the way out.

"Yeah right. I'm the dick. You're Mr. Wonderful and I'm the dick. We've established that. Can we go back to enjoying our day now?"

"Dick," he repeated under his breath.

I stood in the kitchen wondering what the hell just happened.

"So, are you still making breakfast?" I asked confident that it was a legitimate question.

Realizing that the day was not going to go well without Jules present, I took the warmed up souse to her and invited her to come down.

"Are you sure?"

"Definitely. He's in a real mood."

"Do you want some advice?"

"About how to deal with Reed?" I asked the woman who had known him for two days.

"Yeah. I think he thinks you're a little... how do I put it? Entitled?"

"And, why would you think that?" I asked stunned.

"Because I think that? And I think anyone who spends a second with you would think that as well," she said blowing my mind.

"You think I'm entitled?"

"This is less of a "thinking" situation, and more of a "knowing"."

I was shocked. How could anyone think I was entitled?

"When I was a kid I had to do everything for myself. My mother worked all of the time, so I had to cook for myself, clean my own clothes, I had to get myself to school on time. Hell, I even did the yard work. How is that entitled?"

"And, how long ago was that?"

"What's your point?"

"My point is that since you've made a success of yourself, which is definitely very impressive, you might have lost touch with... let's say reality?"

"I've lost touch with reality?"

"Yes," she said confidently.

"Really?"

"Yep."

"You have no idea what you're talking about."

"What's your chef's name?"

"What?"

"Your chef. You've talked to her multiple times. She's someone who you will have to talk to a lot. Reed said her name a few times and I've heard you say it. So, what's her name?"

I paused. "I want to say... Manny?"

"Why would it be Manny? She's a woman."

"Manny could be a..."

"Mildred."

"Right, Mildred. I meant to say, Mildred. What did I say, Manny? I meant Mildred."

"And your driver's name?"

"Look, I don't see what your point is," I told her not liking her as much as I did the night before.

"My point is that maybe if you were a little less dismissive of others and a little more hands-on, Reed might see you in a new light."

With no other options — and believe I searched for one — I decided to take Jules's advice to heart. Maybe I had lost touch a little. It probably wouldn't hurt to take charge a little more. After all, being on top was my natural position.

"We're going out on the boat," I told them after gathering them together. "Jules, you pack a lunch. Reed, you get towels, supplies and the rest. I'll prepare the boat."

"Do you know how to prepare a boat?" Reed asked still being a little bitch.

"It's my boat. I'll prepare the boat," I told him following Jules's advice to the letter.

That left only one problem. I had no idea what "preparing the boat" meant. You just had to get in and turn the key, right?

There turned out to be a little more to it than that, but not much more. I had to find the keys, of course. I had to unsnap the boat's cover and strike an impressive pose waiting for my crew to arrive. Waiting for them, I spotted the fishing gear in the dry dock, so I grabbed them. I hadn't decided what the day would entail, but a good captain was prepared for anything.

"You can't just keep turning the key. You have to prime the engine," Reed said implying that I didn't know what I was doing.

"Of course I have to prime the engine. You think I don't know that? I'm just looking for where the primer is." I also needed to know what the primer was, but Reed didn't need to know that part.

Reed headed to the outboard engine and was about to grab for a rubber ball attached to it when I again remembered Jules's advice.

"No. It's my boat. I'll do it," I told him before rushing back there and squeezing the ball a few times. As I did, I looked over at Jules hoping to get a little acknowledgment for how well I was following her advice. It was weird that it never came.

"That's probably enough," Reed said suddenly.

"I know that," I replied quickly letting go. And, what do you know, when I turned the key again, it started.

From that point on, things went a little smoother. Sure, in the beginning my turns were a little sharp, and my braking was a little abrupt, but I got better. After an hour, I was handling the boat like one of my sports cars. It was actually kind of fun.

Heading over to a nearby island we found a beach. The sand was a beautiful off-white and the crystal clear water gently rolled onto shore as if the island was calmly breathing. It was like out of a dream.

Figuring out how to anchor the boat and then doing it, we headed onto the beach and got comfortable. Jules had packed a picnic basket so we had cheese, meats, crackers, and wine. Those were just the snacks. She also brought a few helpings of Mildred's pea soup and dumplings. We had it a little later with beers.

What I thought was the highlight of the day, however, was when Jules took off her top and laid in the sun. She really wasn't a shy girl. I liked that about her. And, what I liked even more were her superb breasts. Reed liked them too. I could tell by the way he tried to hide his erection. He was such a gentleman in that way.

How crazy was it that he had had sex with a guy, though? How would that have even happened? Did Reed initiate it? Had the other guy? It had to be the other guy, right? Reed didn't have that in him. Or, with guys, was he different?

I didn't know if it was the alcohol or Jules's breast, but pretty soon I was sporting a big one as well. I was an adult so I didn't bother hiding it. Seeing Reed approach the shoreline, I decided to sneak up on him and charge him wrapping my arms around him as I threw both of our bodies into the warm water.

Reed took my playful gesture as it was intended. Surfacing, he laughed and dove at me. Grabbing my waist he dragged me under. It wasn't long before our play turned into wrestling. There was no question which of us was stronger. I was. Flipping him into the air a few times, he wouldn't give up.

"Come on, Reed!" Jules suddenly yelled from the beach.

What was she doing? In spite of the two of them fucking, she was still supposed to be my fiancé.

That was all Reed needed, however. Because after she said what she had, Reed grabbed me and flipped my body into the air. It was impressive.

I wouldn't let him win that easily, though. So, grabbing him and locking his body against mine, we both struggled to get the upper hand until I realized that my hard cock was pushed onto the crack of his ass. Reed must have noticed it too because it was then that he stopped struggling.

I wasn't sure what that meant. Clutching him from behind, my cheek was next to his. He was neither pulling away nor falling into it. And, unsure what I was supposed to do next, I acted without thinking. Without giving it a second thought, I pushed my hard cock onto his ass crack. It was only then that Reed pulled away, stared back at me for a second, then returned to the beach.

Everything in me wanted to know if he was hard too. He was walking away so I couldn't see it. But, he wasn't trying to hide anything so that had to mean something.

I don't know if I would describe things as awkward between him and me after that, but for the next few hours he was certainly quieter than usual. I suggested that we do some fishing, so packing up the boat, we headed out to sea. I hadn't thought to bring bait so we used some of the salami. We had some nibbles but no bites.

Not ready to call an end to our fairly successful day, I next drove the boat between the chains of islands near mine. All but one was completely uninhabited. Most barely had trees. They all had beaches, though. And, driving through the Bimini islands in a speed boat with two of the most gorgeous people that I knew, was a dream.

"We should head back," Reed suggested as the sun got low on the horizon.

"We don't have to," I told him not wanting the day to end.

"How much gas did you put in it?"

"Gas?" I asked suddenly realizing what "preparing the boat" meant. "I filled it up."

"Okay."

"Still, though. It's getting late. We should probably head back," I told him.

Turning the boat around, I realized the other thing that "preparing the boat" probably meant. Because as I looked ahead at all of the islands we had driven by, I discovered that they all looked the same and that a map might have been helpful.

Following our path back turned out not to be as hard as I thought. Before too long, I spotted my island. It was the only one with a mansion looming over it. We were about a half-mile away when Reed said something which I never would have expected.

"You know, Laine, I had my doubts, but you did a good job today."

"What do you mean?"

"This would seem to be outside your element. And I was sure that you were gonna get us lost at sea, but you didn't. I have to say, I'm impressed," he said with a sweet smile.

I can't lie, that made me feel good. And, everything would have been perfect if, at that moment, the boat's engine didn't cough, sputter, and then run out of gas.

Crap!

"What's wrong with the boat?" Jules asked.

"I don't know," I lied.

"It's out of gas," Reed said cynically.

"You don't know that," I challenged.

Reed got up, unscrewed the cap on the engine and looked in. "We're out of gas. I'm curious, Laine, did you fill it up before we left?"

"Fill it up?"

"No, you didn't. Great!"

"I…" I began before realizing there was nothing to say.

"So, what do we do?" Jules asked with us still a quarter-mile from shore.

Reed didn't have to be asked. He was already retrieving the oars and handing them out.

"We're gonna paddle," he said before taking charge.

It was dark and very late by the time we got back to shore, but we did get there. Tying the boat to the dock, Reed got off and headed back to the house. Apparently, he had had enough. Could I blame him? No. This time I really had screwed up, and I couldn't pretend otherwise. He had saved us. In this case, it was Reed who had taken care of me.

Giving Jules a hand emptying the boat, I accompanied her back to the house. Neither of us said anything as we walked. What was there to say? We had all been there. There was no need to discuss it.

As tired as we were, we all immediately headed to bed. I was sure to watch Jules this time. To her credit, she didn't take off to "grab some water" or anything. And we both got to sleep without incident.

Finding her still there the next morning was also a bit of a relief. It was good to know that her promise really was worth something. And when we headed down for breakfast, the worried look on Reed's face told me that he hadn't had a stress reliever during the night.

"What's wrong?" I asked him.

"It's 10 am on a Monday. Did Mildred say anything about not coming into work today?"

"No. Why? Is she not here?"

"No. Which I wouldn't think much of if it wasn't for that," Reed said pointing at the window.

"Bad weather?" I asked him not getting what he was saying.

"Is that all it is?" Reed asked.

"What else would it be?" Jules asked.

"A storm. A hurricane."

"A hurricane?" I asked him surprised by his suggestion.

"It's possible."

I smiled. "Wouldn't that be ironic… you know, considering my nickname."

Reed didn't seem as amused.

Intrigued, I left the kitchen for the front door. The others followed. Standing overlooking the docks we stared out into the increasingly grim sky and watched as the once calm water, bounced the boat against the dock. It was a dark, ominous sight.

Next turning to the trees that surrounded the house, we watched them sway in the wind. It wasn't anything intense but I wondered what might happen if the winds picked up. The breeze was coming from offshore. None of this seemed good. And frankly, as the seriousness of the situation set in, I felt a tightness in my chest thinking about it.

"How do we know what's coming?" I turned back to Reed and asked.

"The Weather Channel?" he suggested as clueless on this topic as I was.

Retreating inside, the three of us made our way to the only TV in the house. It was in the entertainment room at the back of the first floor.

"I assume you have satellite?" Reed asked.

"Yes, I have the full package."

Reed found the remote control and tuned everything to the Weather Channel. It took a while but eventually we heard it.

"Tropical storm Betty which has lingered over the Atlantic for days, has been upgraded to a hurricane and is on a path to hit the Bimini islands in the Bahamas. Although still building, winds are expected to reach close to 100 miles per hour upon landfall with tidal surges as high as 17 feet."

Pulsing heat flushed across my face. There was no way that any of this was good. Staring at the TV, my heart sunk. I had no idea what to do and I couldn't even pretend that I did.

"This is bad, isn't it?" I asked Reed.

"Yeah, this is bad."

"What do we do?" Jules asked us.

"We should head back," I told the group.

"And go where? My place? If I was there I would have had to evacuate."

I thought about his place. He was right. That was no place to be caught in a hurricane.

"A hotel," I suggested.

"We could. But the other option is to wait it out here. This place is a fortress. It has storm shutters, and it's high enough above the waterline. Besides, who's gonna drive the boat back in the storm? The water is getting rougher by the second."

Everything Reed said made my heart thump. This was serious. I had seen the news after a hurricane hit one of these Caribbean islands. It was not pretty. There were deaths. Islands had been razed flat.

"Then, we'll stay," I decided for the group.

"Should we stay?" Jules asked Reed.

"I said we're staying. It's decided," I told her.

"It's probably what's best," he confirmed to my relief. "But, there's a lot of work we'll have to do to prepare."

"Like what?" I asked over the deafening sounds of my heartbeats.

"We need to put up the hurricane shutters. I noticed that there are tracks around the windows for them. We just need to find them. Preparing the house should be our priority, but we'll also need to put the boat into the dry dock."

"How do we do that?" I asked thinking it should be my task.

"I don't know. But, we'll figure that out once we're done with the windows."

Looking up and around, it suddenly dawned on me what made the house so beautiful. It was all of the windows. The walls were practically one big window. And now every one of them had to be covered.

"Did you hear how long we had before landfall?" I asked the others.

"I think they said six hours," Jules explained.

"How did we not get more warning than that? Did you check the weather before we headed out here?" Reed asked me.

"Why would I check the weather? How would I have known to check for a hurricane? I don't live here," I reminded him a little pissed that he was implying that this, too, was my fault.

"I guess it doesn't matter. It is what it is. Did anyone see anything that looked like a storage facility?" Reed asked.

The rest of us shook our head, no.

"Then, let's split up and find it."

I had some idea of where the shutters might be. We had a golf cart, which meant there was a place to charge and store it. If I found that, I would probably find the shutters.

Heading back to the front of the house, I looked around for a garage. There was nothing. But what I did notice was that the asphalt-covered road down to the dock had an offshoot going somewhere behind the roofed dry dock.

Taking the golf cart I followed the path. Tucked away past everything was a small structure. I parked in front of it and looked for a way in. There was no lock. Seeing what was inside made me sweat with panic. Yeah, I had found the shutters. There could have been a hundred of them.

Shit!

Hurrying back to the house, I gathered the others and drove them down. Their reaction was the same as mine. Knowing that we would barely have enough time, we got right to work. The wind was already picking up. So, carrying six-foot by four-foot polycarbonate sails to the house was going to be a challenge.

With the building wind, it took us three hours just to get the shutters to the top of the hill. It took us another hour to figure out which ones went where. That didn't include attaching them. That was a two-person job and required a tool that we only had one of.

"Jules, go around and gather any flashlights or candles you find. The house runs off of a generator but who knows how long it will hold out during the storm," Reed ordered.

"Got it," she said hurrying off.

As the winds got stronger, attaching the shutters became ridiculous. If we held them in anywhere close to the wrong angle, they threatened to rip out of our hands and disappear forever. This was the craziest thing I had ever done in my life. And I started to realize that there was a chance we might die. This could literally be my last few moments alive.

That was when I looked over at Reed. What the hell had I been thinking all of this time? Why hadn't I said anything to him? With my heart pounding, I opened my mouth to say the thing that I had always known that I should have. I couldn't believe that this was finally the moment, but, yeah, it was.

"There's something you need to know, Reed," I told him with my heart thundering from fear and adrenaline.

"What? Is there something else you forgot to tell me that will put our lives at risk?" he said snippily.

"Yeah, kind of, I guess."

"What is it?" he snapped.

"In case we don't make it out of this, I want you to know…"

"What?" Reed said focused on attaching a bolt.

"I love you, Reed."

"Yeah, I love you too."

"No, Reed. I mean that I'm in love with you."

Reed looked up at me and froze.

"I have been for a while."

"Since when?" he asked doubtingly.

"College."

"College?"

"Yeah."

"There's no way. You've treated me like garbage since the day I told you that I was moving here."

"You mean from the day you said that you were leaving the country and probably not coming back? Why would you do that? We had a good thing going and then you left me."

"I didn't leave you. I left that life. I was escaping from under my father's thumb. I needed to figure out who I was without him breathing down my neck."

"You could have joined me in New York," I insisted.

"And do what? Work in an investment firm like you did?"

"Yeah. Why not?"

"Because that's not me, Laine. That's you. That could never have been me."

"Then maybe I might have come with you here if you would have invited me."

"Laine, you know damn well, this place is not you."

"I'm just saying that you didn't have to leave the country. I would have taken care of you, whatever you needed. I would have done anything for you. All you had to do was ask."

Reed lowered his eyes and thought about what I said. He did it until a gust of wind nearly ripped the shutter out of our hands and the first rain droplets hit us both.

"We need to get these shutters on, otherwise we really might not survive the night."

That was not the way I wanted to tell him I loved him and certainly not the response I was hoping for, but it was all out now. As the hours passed, I was beginning to wish that the hurricane would kill us. Well, maybe not everyone. Just me. His lack of response to my declaration was like a vice grip on my heart. It took everything in me not to say fuck it and let Mother Nature have her way. I was heartbroken.

As the hurricane made landfall, we were bolting down the last shutter. We had made it. The winds were more than 50 miles per hour and it was getting difficult to remain standing.

"Oh shit, the boat," I said to Reed who had also forgotten.

Having ended at the back of the house, we hurried through the hammering rain to the front. The waves were an angry beast gnawing its teeth against the rocks. The boat slammed against the dock with ferocity. With ever strike the fiberglass threatened to shatter.

"What do we do?" I asked.

"We let it go," he said resigned.

"You think it'll survive?"

"No. But there's nothing we can do about that now," he said looking at me with fear in his eyes.

"Let's get out of the rain," I told him letting it all go.

Drenched as we entered the house, we looked at each other unsure of what to say. With the shutters on it felt like night. It was barely past midday. It was an eerie feeling.

On top of that, the sound as the rain hit the shutters was like endless buck shots. The monster was doing everything it could to enter, and we had done what we could to keep it at bay. All that was left now was to pray.

Jules rushed into the living room hearing the door close.

"I'll get some towels. I'll be right back," she said again leaving Reed and me alone.

With nothing else that could be done, there was now only one thing on my mind, that I had confessed my love for him. He hadn't responded. What was he thinking? Was this the end of us? Would things never be the same between us again?

I was about to ask him all of this when Jules rushed back in with towels. She had a lot of them and we needed it.

"Take off your clothes," she insisted.

We both complied. Not wanting this to be awkward, I looked away as he undressed and wrapped himself in his towel. Following a step behind him, we both ascended the stairs. After we each headed in our opposite direction, I turned to see if he was looking back at me. He wasn't. As far as I could tell, my confession had been the end of us. The thought of it wrenched at my heart and my will to go on.

Returning downstairs and with nothing else to do, the three of us ate more of Mildred's peas soup and sat glued to the Weather Channel. We weren't learning anything new but none of us dared to change it to anything else. The howling outside was getting louder. It sounded like the house was breathing. In one moment it was taking an ungodly inhale. Then, just as quickly, it would breathe out in a siren's wail.

Snap! The lights went out. Everything was dark and the sounds were magnified.

"Where are the candles?" I asked Jules.

"They're right here," she said scrambling in the dark.

The scratching of a lighter joined the cacophony. With it came a single light that illuminated Jules's face. The flickering made her skin glow. As she leaned down to the candle getting a little closer to me, I realized that it wasn't her skin which was glowing. It was the tears rolling down her cheeks.

"I'm scared," she said with the handful of candles lit in front of us.

I opened my arms inviting her into them and she came. Tucked by my side on the couch, she looked over at Reed. That was his invitation and he accepted it.

With both of us wrapping Jules in our arms, I could feel Reed's skin touching mine. It was so intimate, so much like when we were kids. The screeching winds made Jules's grip around me tighter. Drawing Reed in as she moved, I found his face inches from mine.

I could feel Reed's warm breath caress my face. It was making it harder for me to breathe. I wanted so desperately to lean over and feel his lips on mine that my soul ached. I could feel us getting closer with each of our breaths. It was too much for me. I threatened to pull away until… our lips touched for the first time.

Our kiss was like nothing I had ever experienced. It was warm caramel pulled in endless combinations as it drained its way through my brain. My skin was on fire. He was letting me kiss him. If the man I had loved for so long had let me do this, what else would he allow?

Reaching over Jules, I grabbed Reed by the back of his neck and kissed him like I had always dreamed. Parting my lips, he did the same. In search of his tongue, I found it. Together our two tongues danced. It was everything I had ever dreamed it would be, maybe more.

The two of us kissed and kissed until my cock was brick hard. Having realized it, I didn't feel the uncomfortable constriction which usually accompanied it. I also no longer felt Jules's arms on me. There was a reason for both. While I had been lost in Reed's embrace, Jules had unzipped my pants and had pulled my cock out. With one of her small hands barely gripping it, she was caressing the head of it with her tongue.

This was happening. There was no stopping us now. We could all get what we wanted. I could have Reed. Reed could have Jules. And Jules could have either of us.

Letting loose my restraints, I grabbed Reed's shirt ripping it off his body. He moved his arms wanting me too. Next, I unbuttoned his pants. With him lifting his hips helping me, I unzipped him and stripped him bare.

Knowing what I had wanted to do for so long, I brushed Jules aside, pushed Reed back and reached for his perfect cock. I had seen it but had never touched it. Reaching for it, I marveled at what it looked like erect.

Leaning down, I rubbed its length across my cheek. It felt glorious. Then finally when I opened my mouth allowing the ridge of his head to slide across my lip before plunging it in, I felt complete for the first time in my life.

Taking hold of my best friend with two hands, I pushed the tip of him onto the back of my throat. I wished that it would open up so that he could fuck me. It didn't, though, and that was okay. Instead, I decided that I would have to fuck him.

Opening my eyes and looking up, I found Jules. She was now naked leaning over him kissing him like I had once done. It was beautiful to watch. I knew how much this meant to him. I wanted him to have more.

"Fuck her," I whispered while gently caressing his balls.

I didn't have to tell either of them twice. As soon as I said it, Reed pulled out of my grip allowing Jules to lie under him and then spread her legs readying her for his cock.

Placing my hand on his naked ass, I got low to watch the moment up close. His manhood entered her pussy as if it were returning home. Her stilted breaths were the reaction. The sight was beautiful.

Feeling a rumbling in my chest, I slid my thumb to his hole and rubbed. His slow thrusts into Jules added to my pressure. And when my yearning ache became too much to ignore, I replaced my thumb with my tongue. It was Reed's turn to moan. It was the best sound I ever heard.

As Reed's measured thrusts continued, tasting the inside of him was no longer enough. I felt lightheaded I wanted him so badly. Getting up I placed the length of my cock along his crack. As he thrust, my dick rubbed against his hole. His moans increased. It was as I could no longer hold out that I heard Reed utter the words that I had, for so long, dreamed to hear.

"Fuck me," he muttered through panicked breaths.

Dripping with cum, I took him immediately. Placing the tip of me on his hole, he paused as I pulled him apart. He might have been fucked before, but not by someone of my size. I could tell.

The force of it made his legs wobble. I had grip his waist to hold him up. Then, when I had finally reached the depth of him and he had caught his breath, he plunged himself deep into Jules fucking himself as he did.

Penetrating the man I had loved for so long was everything I ever wanted it to be. I was sure to take care of him as it happened. Guiding him with my hand, I started his thrusts off slowly. But cranking his hip like a locomotive on the run, I fucked him faster and harder until, like a train, each of our whistles blew.

"Ahhh," Jules squealed quivering like a leaf below us.

"Ohhh," Reed bellowed locking his hips as he did.

And when I came, exploding my cum into his willing ass, it was with the feeling that, after a lifetime of searching, I had finally found my way home. I loved this man and would do anything in the world I had to to take care of him. I was going to do whatever I had to to keep him.

Chapter 4

Reed

Well, that was unexpected. But, lying there still in Jules and with Laine's cock firmly planted in me, I had never felt more complete. I wouldn't say that this was what I had always wanted. It was more that this was a surprise that I didn't know I would love.

The only other guy I had been with was Juan. He was here on a fishing trip with his buddies. That man had a lot of sexual energy. And once I got caught in the gravity of his desire, there was nothing I could do to escape it.

It wasn't like I hadn't thought about being with a guy before him. Even before meeting him I would have described myself as fully bi-curious. And my time with Juan had lived up to my expectations. He had taken the lead and had done to me what Laine just had. It was an incredible feeling. But, it wasn't anywhere close to what had just happened.

It took me a long time to admit that my father wasn't completely wrong when he referred to Laine as my boyfriend. Looking back on it, Laine probably was. We had never had sex or had even kissed. But I had been obsessed with him. I had wanted to spend every free moment with him. And when I was with him, I connected with him by talking about Jules.

I don't know, maybe it was my way of relating to him. Laine definitely slept around. After every party at college, he went home with a different girl. It was insane. I had no idea how he could do it. And, obviously, a guy like that could never have feelings for another dude. So instead, I spent every waking moment with him talking about something that made the two of us more alike.

Don't get me wrong, it wasn't that I didn't have a thing for Jules. I did. She was the object of almost all of my sexual fantasies. It was just that I wanted to have sex with Jules and have Laine wrap me in his arms.

That difference wasn't something that college-aged me could understand. So instead, I just went nuts. I became obsessed with them both in different ways and then had to come up with an explanation to my conservative judge father who fought against the enforcement of the hate crime laws.

Did I move to the island to run from my feelings for Laine? Looking back on it, yeah. I was devastated when he decided to move to New York. After he left, I cried myself to sleep for weeks.

My father, who knew what was going on before I did, was brutal to me after that. Not only would he call me the worst names he could think of, but he threatened to disown me.

I needed to get as far away as possible. So, taking my meager trust fund, I moved to Bimini devoting my life to helping others the way I wished someone would have helped me. After a few years, it no longer felt like I was running. The place grew on me. Bimini became the home I never had.

As time passed, I thought about both Jules and Laine less. It helped that Laine would visit and do nothing but make me feel bad about my choices. By the time that Juan showed up, I was ready to move on. I am so grateful to have had my time with that gorgeous stranger. But, it in no way compared to being with Jules and Laine now.

"Do you two want to head upstairs?" Laine asked. "Our bed would be more comfortable."

"Sure," I replied not caring where I was as long as I was with them.

"Okay," Jules said making our move official.

By that point, Laine's incredibly thick member had shrunken out of my ass while mine had done the same from Jules. Unpeeling from on top of each other, the only other sound was the howling of the wind. It was haunting. I had only been in one other hurricane since moving to the islands, but this one was far worse.

Not only were the winds projected to be harder, but the tidal surge was predicted to be higher. Much higher. My only hope was that everyone back home had had more time than we had had to prepare.

It was hard to judge anything about the hurricane being in this house, however. Not only was this place 30 feet above sea level, but it had metal on the windows. The rain sounded like scattered shots against it. If I just went by that, I would guess that the world was ending. So instead of worrying about it, I decided to lose myself in the best experience of my life.

Repositioning ourselves on Laine and Jules's bed, I found myself between the two. All we did for the next few hours was make love. With Laine's leg intertwined with mine, I would make out with his fiancé. And with Jules's hands reaching around and stroking my cock, I would take hold of Laine's monster while he slowly kissed every inch of my face.

There was certainly a lot more fucking too. Laine fucked me again and again, while I took turns going down on the two of them and fucking Jules. It was weird that the two of them never fucked. But I guess it was an invited-guest situation where the two hosts indulged themselves with the newbie. Whatever the reason, I was okay with it. In fact, I felt lucky just to be invited into their bed.

Without a clock, it was hard to tell what time we all finally fell asleep. With the storm shutters covering the windows, it was impossible to tell what time it was when we got up. I felt well-rested so it had to be at least seven hours. That brought up another question, why did the battering on the windows sound just as intense as it did the day before?

On average hurricanes travel at 20 miles per hour and are 300 miles across. I learned that the first time I got caught in one. That meant that the typical hurricane took fifteen hours to pass. It first hit us at 2 pm yesterday. It was now the next morning. Shouldn't it have already passed?

"Is everyone awake?" Laine asked to our confirmation. "Should we get something to eat?"

"We probably still have leftovers," Jules informed us.

We were all slow to get dressed and head downstairs. The kitchen was as dark as everywhere else. The fridge was still cold and the stove was still working so we warmed the remainder of the souse. Souse always got better the longer it sat, so at this point, breakfast was amazing.

"How long do these things usually last?" Laine eventually asked.

"I would have said fifteen hours, but maybe this one is bigger than usual. Does anyone know the time?"

Luckily there was a grandfather clock in the back room.

"It's 4 pm? Is that right?" I exclaimed.

"Maybe. Who can tell in the dark?" Jules replied.

No matter the size, 26 hours was a long time for a hurricane to last. This was not good.

"I want to see outside," I told them starting to feel on edge.

"You think that's a good idea?" Laine countered.

"I don't know, but I have to see."

"You want to try the front door?"

The three of us crossed the house to the foyer. The door racked back and forth as if the devil himself was trying to get in. I could imagine opening it and never being able to get it closed. More than that, the change of pressure could rip the roof off the house.

The homes in the Bahamas were built to survive up to 150 mile-an-hour winds. But roofs were always the most vulnerable part. Even when nothing else was done to the house, roofs were known to be deposited a mile away when the home was suddenly depressurized.

"Any way we could open one of the shutters on the second floor?" I asked them.

Those shutters were built in so Jules had been responsible for closing them.

"Maybe. I don't know how much we should, though. The wind made them really hard to shut once it got going."

"Let's do that then. I have to see what's going on."

At the end of the hall upstairs was the window facing the dock. The wind had been coming from that direction but I needed to risk it. Standing in front of the window with Laine and Jules standing further back, I took hold of the lever that locked the shutters into place. The pressure against it was fiercely fighting me from opening it up.

When it did open, what followed was the rapid flexing of the window's panes. They expanded and collapsed like lungs. There was no question they were going to explode. But before they did, I had to look out to see what surrounded us.

Peering quickly, what I found was devastating. The dock and the twelve-foot tall dry dock were both gone. There was nothing around us but water. I leaned looking to the left and right. There were once tall trees there which should have poked above the surface. There was nothing. It was like the island had sunk and all that was left was the house.

Hearing the glass inches from my face begin to crack, I tore myself from the desolate view and did everything I could to close the shutters. As hard as it was to open, it was even harder to shut. I fought and fought until, like an explosion, the shutter snapped into place sending me tumbling to the ground.

"Are you alright?" Laine yelled as the two of them rushed to my side.

I was startled. What had just happened? I looked around. There was glass everywhere.

"Yeah, I'm fine," I quickly reassured them.

"You're bleeding," Jules told me.

Feeling a sting, I touched my face. My hand came back bloody.

"Careful, there's glass," Jules warned me. "Let's get you cleaned up," she said before she and Laine helped me up.

"What did you see out there?" Laine asked me as Jules carefully picked the shards out of my skin.

What was I supposed to tell him? To me, it looked like the end of the world. It looked like the only thing that was left on planet earth was us and this house. That couldn't be what I saw, though. And there was no way I could further worry my friends who had already been freaked out beyond reason.

"There's damage," I told them drastically underselling the apocalypse.

"How much damage?" Laine asked.

I looked at him. "You'll need a landscaper."

"Okay," he replied confused. "But, are we going to die?"

"No," I reassured them wishing that someone would reassure me. "The hurricane probably just slowed down on top of us or something. It happens," I reminded myself.

"So, how much longer do you think it'll last?" Jules asked giving me a bandage and gesturing for me to apply pressure.

I did the math. The longest I had ever heard of a hurricane lasting was a day and a half. "By tomorrow morning," I told them giving them the worst possible scenario.

"Tomorrow morning?" Laine protested.

"At the latest. Maybe sooner, I just don't know. Don't worry, either way we'll be fine."

My words did seem to calm them though they did nothing for me. As the day continued, the two of them engaged in friendly conversation even joking around now and again. There was nothing I could say to join in.

Situating the group so I could monitor the front door, I kept half of my attention on it. It truly was the end of the world if water started seeping in under it. At thirty feet above sea level that had to mean that the island was sinking. I was no geologist, but what other explanation would there be?

With my face scabbed and tender, nothing happened between us when we went to bed that night. Again finding myself between them, I was the only one not to sleep. Apparently, they both snored. It wasn't horrible but I did hear it over the pounding rain, so…

By the next morning I had managed to get an hour or two of sleep. The good thing was that when I awoke, the pounding had stopped. There were still light ticks on the metal shutters, but that could have been explained by light rain. Otherwise, the house was deathly quiet.

"Reed, are you awake?" Laine asked. I wondered how he knew.

"Yeah."

"It's morning. Do you think it's over?"

"It could be the eye," I told them.

"What's that?" Jules asked.

Laine replied, "It's the center of the hurricane, right?" he confirmed with me.

"Yeah. I doubt it, though. It would be one hell of a hurricane if it was."

"So, what do we do now?" Laine asked again.

I opened my eyes. The movement shot bolts of pain across my face. It was the cuts that were doing it.

"We should give it some time before we go out to check. I'd say at least an hour."

"And if it's gone, then we can get out of here?"

I wondered how he thought we were going to do that then remembered that he hadn't seen what I had. "Yeah," I reassured him not seeing the point in telling him now.

I'm not a religious man, but for the next hour, I prayed. I didn't see a way out of this. We were basically living the live version of the movie Castaway, you know, if along with Wilson, Tom Hanks had a multi-million dollar home.

"It's been an hour," Laine told me some time later.

"How do you know?" I asked him knowing we were nowhere near the grandfather clock.

"Just trust me. I know it's been an hour."

"Okay, then. Let's go outside," I said with my heart sinking.

Opening the door, I was fully prepared to find nothing but ocean. We didn't. The water had receded and there was still an island. What Laine and Jules weren't prepared for was that it had been stripped bare. The grass, the asphalt path to the house, and the trees were all gone. With the oversaturated ground, it looked like we were in the middle of a marsh.

"Where's the dock?" Jules asked.

"Where's the boat?" Laine replied.

"There," I told them after looking around and finding the boat upside down and five feet from the house.

"How did it get there?" Laine wondered aloud.

"There was a tidal surge. When I looked out, all of this was underwater."

"So, can we get it back into the water?" Laine asked.

"Can you lift a boat?" I rebutted.

"If I have to."

"Oh, and do you have a spare engine. Looks like we'll need one," I said gesturing to the back of the boat where the engine used to be.

"What does this mean?" Jules asked.

"It means we're fucked," Laine exclaimed.

"Yep, we're fucked," I confirmed truly not seeing a way out of this.

"What do we do?" Jules asked the both of us.

I looked at Laine in search of an answer. Hers was a good question.

"Do you think the satellite is still working?" Laine asked me.

"Even if it was, how would we get power?" I countered.

"We could try and fix the generator," Jules suggested.

"Has anyone seen the generator? Does anyone know where it is?" I asked.

"Wasn't that the humming we heard when we found the shutters?" Laine suggested.

I turned looking down the hill. There were once trees hiding the storage shack. There weren't anymore. More than that, there was no longer a storage shack.

"We really are screwed, aren't we?" Laine said beginning to wilt.

I didn't want to agree with him. I wanted to tell them that everything was going to be okay. But who even knew that we were out here? Monty did. Was there any chance that his boat survived the hurricane considering the swell that came with it? Very little.

I opened my mouth about to confirm it when a noise crested the sound of the ocean. I looked around wondering what it was. I couldn't tell.

"Do you hear that?" I asked the others.

They listened for a moment and then heard it too.

"I don't know," Laine said. "It sounds like a..."

"Helicopter!" Jules proclaimed.

All of our attention quickly shifted to the sky. The sky was still grey, but in the distance was a spot of red. As we stared, it got closer.

"It's a rescue helicopter!" I told them. "It had to be Monty. He sent this for us. See, that is why you learn people's names," I said elated.

Running to the barren backyard, the three of us waved our hands and yelled. As they approached, it was clear that they saw us. Throwing my arms around my two friends, I could have cried. When the helicopter landed on the cleared open field, a man ran out to greet us.

"Mr. Toros?"

"Yes, that's me."

"Your office sent us to look for you. Do you need rescuing?"

"Yes, we do!" Laine shouted before turning to me. "See, that's why you have money."

I stepped back shaken. I had nothing to say to that.

"Is there anything you need to gather?" the man in the orange jumpsuit ask.

"We'll gather our stuff," Jules declared before leading us away.

Quickly packed and leaving the island, the man in orange examined my face. "It's just scratches," he said.

"I know," I told him. "Where are we going?"

"Fort Lauderdale," the young, bearded man said.

"We can't go there," I told them.

"Why not?"

"We need to get back to Bimini. They might need our help."

The rescuer looked at Laine telling me that they would do what Laine wanted them too.

"Laine, you need to take me home. They might need me. We need to go there first."

Laine looked at me considering it.

"Please, Laine," I begged, though I shouldn't have had too.

"Take us back to Bimini," Laine told the man.

"Take us to Bimini," the man relayed to the captain over his headset.

It only took us a few minutes to again be over familiar ground. What we found, though, was beyond belief. I had known this place. There were many mornings when I had circled the island on my bicycle and had gotten home in time to have breakfast. I knew its roads and buildings intimately. What I was now looking down at was a barren wasteland.

It looked like a bomb had gone off. Homes and buildings that I had walked by many times were gone. They had been wiped off the face of the earth. And all that was left of any of it were shards of wood and boats that were deposited at the exact center of the island.

"Oh my god," Jules said stunned.

"The hurricane shelter is north. Head north," I told them.

With my heart about to shatter, something familiar entered my view. The northern end of the island was where the hotels were. To my relief, they were still standing. It was also where the shelter was.

"Land there," I told them.

The man again looked at Laine. Laine looked hesitant.

"We have to go there," I told him.

"Land," he ordered.

Hearing the helicopter, dozens of people poured out of the building. It took the pilot a while to find a place to land. As soon as we touched ground, I ran out. I scanned the faces for anyone familiar. I saw a number of people I knew. But, the faces I was really looking for were the Johnsons. The couple was in their eighties. I had to make sure that they were alright.

Leaving the throng I entered the hotel. Heartbroken souls were everywhere. Spotting Vernon, one of the guys who helped me take care of Mr. Johnson's yard, I ran over and grabbed him.

"Have you seen the Johnsons? Are they alright?"

He looked at me as his brow folded into misery. He began to cry.

"What happened?" I asked, my heart pounding in my throat.

Without a word, Vernon dragged me out of the hotel into the hotel's convention room. Cots lined every inch of the space. Weaving through them, he led me to Thelma. She was sprawled lifeless across the canvas. She looked to be in shock.

"Thelma, where are your parents? Where's your baby?"

She didn't move. It was Vernon who finally spoke up.

"Oh Reed, it was awful. Mr. and Mrs. Johnson refused to leave their place and Thelma decided to stay to take care of them."

"No!" I exclaimed not believing what I was hearing. Tears began pouring down my cheeks.

"Thelma told us that when the tide came in, the yard flooded first. That's when they realized that they needed to be rescued and headed to the roof. She said that they were there for hours in the rain waiting. The water got so deep that they saw a shark swimming around their yard. A shark, Reed! A shark!"

"What happened, Vernon?"

"Seeing that, for some reason, Thelma decided that she needed to get more baby formula. Maybe she thought the world was ending or something. So she gave the baby to Mr. Johnson and swam back into the house. She said she was gone for less than five minutes. But when she got back, Mr. and Mrs. Johnson and her baby were gone.

"They were gone, Reed! They gone! Nobody has seen them since."

My heartbreak and devastation were complete. My soul had been torn apart. I looked down at Thelma as the tears streamed down my face. I didn't know what to do or say. All I felt was raw emotion.

"Reed, we gotta go," I heard someone say behind me.

I turned seeing Laine. I was too dazed to understand him. He grabbed me by the shoulder.

"Reed, we have to go!" he said shaking me awake.

"What are you talking about going? We need to stay. These people need our help."

"There's nothing you can do here." Clutching my arm, he pulled me away from Vernon and Thelma. "Look, things are going to get bad here. We need to get out of here. I have all the money in the world. Let's go to

New York and forget that any of this ever happened. Let's go anywhere. It could be your choice. You, Jules, and me, we could be eating dinner in Spain by nightfall. We can go anywhere. We just can't stay here."

It was then that I looked around spotting Jules behind him. It felt surreal. I felt disconnected from my body. "I can't do that," I said without thinking.

"Why not?" Laine implored.

"Because these people are my family."

"No, Reed. These people aren't your family. I am." Laine gestured back at Jules. "We could be."

It was then that something registered in my mind for the first time since I had heard it.

"Jules, what temp agency did you work for?"

She responded with a jolt. "What temp agency did I work for? You mean when I met Laine?"

"Yeah. Was it Temporary Temps?"

"Yeah. How did you know that?"

"You know he owns that company, right?"

Jules turned to Laine. "You own Temporary Temps?"

Laine didn't respond to her. "How did you know that?" he asked me.

"It was the first company you purchased. I remember you said to me that the economy was going to change and that companies were going to start relying on freelancers. I remember it because you turned out to be right."

"You own Temporary Temps?" Jules said washing the thought around in her mind.

"You don't know what family is," I told Laine suddenly sure of it. "You don't know what love is. Everything is just a transaction to you. You need to get out of my life."

"I don't know what love is?" Laine fired back. "At least I haven't spent half of my life hiding from it. At least I didn't leave the country running from it. You know what Laine, you're pathetic. I don't know why I ever cared about you. Jules, let's go."

Laine began to walk away, but she stayed put.

"Jules, I said, let's go."

"But…"

"Do you care about your mother?"

Jules's eyes snapped towards Laine.

"If you care about her, get on that helicopter now."

It was only then that Jules moved. Allowing her eyes to briefly meet mine, she quickly looked away and followed Laine out. It didn't take long to hear the roar of the helicopter as it took off and flew away. A part of me expected one of them to run back into the room and into my arms. No one did. They were both gone.

Chapter 5

Jules

As the helicopter took off, I stared across the aisle at Laine. His face was twisted with anger as he peered out of the window. It was then that it truly hit me, I didn't know who he was. Had he just threatened my mother's life? Was he some sort of psychopath?

I hadn't known that he owned Temporary Temps. What did that mean? Bill had said that they had ended my assignments because of "corporate". Laine was corporate. As the owner of the company, there was no one more corporate than him. Had Laine been the one to order that my assignments end? Why? At that point, I hadn't seen him in years. Had this all been his plan?

"What did you mean that if I cared about my mother, I'd leave with you?"

"Don't overthink it," Laine said still not looking at me.

"Overthink what? That you gave my mother cancer?"

Laine whipped his head towards me with genuine shock on his face. "What? You think I gave your mother cancer? What are you, insane?"

"I don't know!" I shouted. "You were insane enough to get me fired. You were insane enough to make me desperate so I would accept your bat-shit crazy proposal."

"And who benefited from that? You needed money. Did you really think that you would get it working a temp assignments earning $15 an hour? I rescued you! You think anyone else would have paid you $200,000 for anything? You should be getting on your knees and thanking me for what I did for you. I gave your mother cancer? I saved your mother's life!"

Well, it was official. I had just spent the week with a psychopath. Was he trying to justify what he did? There was no justifying it. He tricked me into helping him lie to Reed. And then he forced me to abandon him when Reed needed someone the most. If there was anyone eviler than Laine, I had never met them. All I could do now was watch him like a hawk and pray that he didn't kill me to remove the evidence of what had happened.

It was a long hour as we flew back to Florida. It's amazing how tense your shoulders get when you're making sure someone doesn't kill you. I survived, though. In fact, Laine never even looked at me.

When we landed, I was about to flee the helicopter when he beat me to it. Standing in the doorway, he didn't make eye contact as he said,

"My people will arrange your flight back to California. Your money will be sent to the bank account on file at the agency."

And then, with that, he left the helicopter and walked out of my life. I had once asked him why they called him Hurricane Laine. Now I knew. It was because he was as destructive as any storm.

I still wasn't sure what had gone on and why he had done it. But all I cared about now was getting home and getting what he had promised me.

My trip back to Los Angeles was set within minutes of me stepping onto the tarmac. It was a first-class seat which probably cost a year's salary at minimum wage.

I had never traveled in first-class before. On a cross country non-stop flight it was really worth it. Okay, I don't know if it was worth whatever it cost for a last-minute reservation, but it felt quite luxurious.

Grabbing my bags off of the conveyor belt I was looking for the exit when I saw something else I wasn't expecting. The guy who had driven me to the airport was holding a sign with my name on it. He had been sent to pick me up. Deciding that I needed Laine out of my life for good, I lowered my head and walked by him. When I was on the street, I flagged a taxi and headed home.

Without question, this had been the craziest few days of my life. I was going to be scarred forever. The scene on Bimini was like a disaster movie. Considering what we went through at Laine's place, I couldn't imagine what they had experienced on flat land.

"I need a vacation," I said with realization.

"Pardon me?" the taxi driver replied.

"Sorry. Nothing," I told him remaining quiet for the rest of the trip home.

My mother's eyes were a wonderful sight to see. I had imagined myself falling into her arms in tears. I didn't. I chalked it up to my plucky resilience. You can knock me down, but I will get back up. And, if I could survive having someone like Laine in my life for a week, I could survive anything.

I don't know if I was surprised or not, but a few days later I checked my bank account. The $200,000 he had promised me was there. At least with that, he had been a man of his word. Too bad he had been a lying, psychopath with everything else.

I have to say, paying my mother off for my student loans did feel good. It was also a shot of life in my mother's arm. Everything in our household became lighter after that.

After paying off my mother, I still had $50,000 to do with whatever I wanted. Now that my mother no longer needed me, I considered taking a real vacation. I had certainly earned it. I could barely imagine anyone who had earned it more.

Unfortunately, it was around then that the images from Hurricane Betty became ever-present on the news. The number of deaths was said to be 50 and rising. And most of them had come from Bimini, an island with a population of 2000. It was declared a humanitarian crisis.

The more days that passed, the harder it got for me to believe that I had been there. What was even harder to believe than that was that I knew someone who was still there. I kept trying to imagine what Reed was going through.

Did he have food or water? Where was he sleeping? Had his house been destroyed? It had to have been, right? And what had happened to the delightful elderly couple he had introduced Laine and me to.

"Thelma with the mangos," I remembered with a chuckle.

As more time passed since my dramatic escape, the more I thought of Reed and the unthinkable.

"Mom, what would you say if I told you that I was considering going back to Bimini?"

"The island hit by the hurricane?"

"Yeah," I confirmed.

"Why?"

"I don't know. It's just starting to feel like something I should do."

My mother looked at me with a knowing smile. "So tell me again about Reed."

I wasn't sure why she had asked me that. This didn't have to do with Reed. This was about helping people in need of help. At least, I hoped it was.

"Reed is... I don't know, an amazing guy."

"Why?"

"I don't know. He just is." I could tell her that when Laine asked him to leave with us, he stayed. Who does something like that? "There are people who run out of burning buildings, and people who run into them to save others. Reed's the type who runs into them," I decided to say.

"He sounds like a good guy."

"Yeah, he does," I said thinking about him more.

As the days went by, I didn't think about Reed less.

"Mom, what if I told you I was really thinking about going back to Bimini and helping with hurricane clean up?"

"I would ask you if you were sure," my mother replied.

"And, if I said that I was?"

"I would tell you that I might have already asked around about it for you."

"And?" I asked my mother both terrified and excited.

"As you know, I've started the process of returning to work. It turns out that the studio has a charitable organization involved with hurricane relief. Apparently, we've shot a few movies there over the years and the studio feels that it should be giving back."

"Okay. What does that mean?" I asked sitting at my mother's side on the couch.

"It means that they are looking for volunteers who would be willing to go down there."

My heart pounded hearing my mother's words. I was awash in emotions. I didn't know what to think. All I was sure about was that I needed to hear more.

"Did you tell someone that I might be interested?"

"How would I have known that you might be interested?" Mom said with a knowing smirk.

"Mom! Because you know me," I insisted.

"You're right, Honey. I do know you. And, yes, I let them know that you might be interested. Here's the phone number," she said handing me a slip of paper from the end table.

I held the paper in front of me and stared at it. What was I looking at? Was this my way of giving back, or was this my way back into Reed's life?

What did I even know about Reed other than he was gorgeous, hot, a fantastic lover, and a good human being? Past that I knew nothing. At that moment I was having a hard time remembering what other qualities mattered, but I was sure there had to be something.

What did start to dawn on me as I stared at the slip was something else. My recent relationship with Reed had been based on a lie. I was not Laine's fiancé. And, as much as I wanted to hate Laine for that as well, it was something that I had to take responsibility for.

After Reed and I had slept together for the first time, I wanted to tell Reed the truth. I asked Laine if I could tell him. And then, instead of simply doing what was right, I chose Laine's money. After I slept with Reed the second time, I chose the same thing.

I could sit back and say that Laine was the devil tempting me with his false idols. But, the money helped. My and my mother's life would never be the same thanks to it. Laine obnoxiously claimed that he had saved my mother's life. That was obviously self-aggrandized bullshit, but it truly had been a life preserver tossed at us as we drowned in a sea of despair.

We really did need the money. And, if I were forced to make the choice again, I would choose the same.

So, where did that leave me with Reed? I don't know. Certainly, I didn't owe Laine anything else. My debt to him was paid in full. There was no need for me to keep on lying to Reed. Which meant that, if I did see Reed again, I would have to come clean.

What would he think of me after that? Would even a friendship be possible? I had helped Laine trick and deceive him. And as much as I regretted it, I was complicit. I would have to accept whatever consequences followed.

Was I willing to do that? Yes. Was Reed really worth the potential humiliation? I didn't know. But staring at the phone number in front of me, I decided I was going to find out.

Calling and then meeting with the charity's organizers, I was given a rundown of everything that would happen once we got to Bimini. The organization would be supplying emergency housing for all of the volunteers. I learned quickly that "emergency housing" was code for tents. They were big tents, but they were still tents.

Some of us would be housed in whatever unused homes could be found in the area. Whitfield, the group's chief organizer, liked me and told me he would put me in a vacation property they located. There was a hole in the roof, but fixing the roof would be the first thing the group would tackle.

After getting shots that I didn't have to get when I was going there for vacation, I packed my most rugged summer attire and met the group at the airport. My body tingled as I thought about what it would be like to see Reed again.

He was going to have so many questions for me. I wasn't looking forward to that part. But seeing him felt incredible. We had only spent a few days together — you know, not including the four years of college — but I was already beginning to miss him intensely. I only hoped that he was feeling the same about me.

Taking the flight across the continent was uneventful. What was quite unique was our transfer from the airport to the Port of Miami. Apparently, the Bimini airport was washed away during the hurricane. We would have to take a boat to the island. It was all pretty intense. I was beginning to wonder what I had gotten myself into.

As the Bimini port came into view, my feeling of dread only got worse. There had to be a thousand people waiting at the dock. The sight was overwhelming.

"What's going on?" I asked Whitfield.

"The island's out of food and the only way the locals get supplies is from the ships that come in. The first thing we'll do is set up a distribution chain from the boat. Hopefully, we'll be able to hand out 300 gallons of water in the first hour. Our second priority would be to start cooking up hot meals. We'll hand that out next."

Listening to him and seeing the throngs of people, I realized that I had had no idea what I was getting myself into. I had been here weeks earlier. In the short time since I had left, the beautiful paradise had been transformed into a refugee camp. How could things change so quickly?

Overwhelmed and shaken, the only thing I could do was do what I was told. As the boat approached the dock we were asked to line between the boat's cargo hold door and the pallets of water. Whitfield said that we were doing this to avoid a riot. If we could hand out the water fast enough, the desperate people wouldn't storm the ship and strip it bare.

Seriously, what the hell had I gotten myself into? This was insanity.

Shutting up and doing what I was told, I stood in line and waited. When the cargo hold's door was opened and the endless sea of faces appeared in front of us, bottles of water were passed to me before I passed it to the next person in rapid succession.

There was no time to think about anything. Receive it, pass it along. Receive it, pass it along. I couldn't tell you how long I did that for. But the brief moments when I could look up, I could see that it was working.

The guys at the end of the line would ask the person who received the water to step aside, but so many times they didn't. They were too busy lifting the bottle to their lips and desperately pouring it down their throat. When was the last time any of these people had drinking water?

After what had to be an hour or two, the mad rush for water finally slowed. The crowd which had packed the space in front of the ship had dispersed. It was only now that Whitfield thought it safe enough to set up the cooking station on the dock.

The work we did that day was endless. I had never carried so much in my life. I had thought that moving days were intense. Picture that and add the slightest possibility that if you didn't move fast enough, you would be trampled to death in a stampede.

It was amazing how much calmer things became after we started serving food. People stood around eating the plates of chili and rice like it was the most incredible feast they had ever had. Folks came back for seconds and thirds and we kept giving it to them. And when they realized that we weren't going to run out and that we would still be there in the morning, they began to leave.

"Thank you!" one grateful local said. "You saved our lives," said another.

After the tenth person said it, I was reduced to tears. After the fiftieth person said it, my spine had stiffened ready to do absolutely anything I had to to get this community back on its feet.

Exhausted, I and a few others were transported to the place where we would be staying. Other than the gaping hole in the roof and the tree branch lodged within it, it looked nice. It looked like a lot of detail had been paid to the home's design. I was sure that I couldn't afford to stay there under usual circumstances. That was not now, however.

The second day was much calmer than the first. I was collected at sunrise to help at the dock cooking and distributing breakfast. I was happy about the assignment. I figured that everyone on the island would filter through the line by the end of the shift. If everyone did, it meant that Reed would as well.

My stomach churned as I thought about seeing him. I saw the state that the other locals were in. Would he look just as bad? And, what would he say when he saw me. I had so much to tell him.

There was good news and bad news by the end of the breakfast shift. The good news was that everything went smoothly. The friendly faces that I had seen on my first trip there had returned. There were so many smiles.

The bad news was that none of those friendly faces was that of Reed's. I was hoping he had just skipped breakfast and that I would see him at lunch. But when lunch came and went and he didn't show up, I began to wonder if I would see him at all. I wondered if he was still alright.

"We aren't the only food distribution center on the island. The government set up one at the shelter."

"You mean the hurricane shelter?" I said remembering where we had landed the helicopter.

That had been where we had left Reed. That was probably where he still was. I briefly considered asking for a transfer there. But quickly I realized that I had made a commitment to help the hungry people at the dock. I was here for them. They needed me. And I would do whatever was necessary to help.

As the days passed, things settled into a degree of normalcy. I had begun to attach names to some of the friendly faces. Some were even sharing stories they had heard about what had happened during the storm. There were a few which were terrifyingly horrific.

As much as I could relate, I dared not share my story. For the most part, my time was spent with Reed's body consuming mine. My memories of the hurricane were intense, but for a whole different reason than everyone else's.

"Jules!" Whitfield called.

"What's up?"

"We're going to be changing up our distribution strategy. We want people to be able to work on their homes. So, instead of making everyone come to us, were going to take the meals to them.

"Here's a map of the island. I want you to start asking people where they live and where they're working. Tell them that we'll start delivering the food to them."

"Got it. I'm on it."

Looking at the map I got my first lay of the land. The island wasn't very big. It was easy to spot the airport and the road we took to Reed's place. That was on the southern island. I could also see that the main shelter was in Alice Town on the northern island. It was less than two miles away from where we were docked.

After asking enough people I got a clear idea of where everyone's home was. There weren't that many places where people lived. After sharing it with Whitfield, he told me,

"You're going to head up the mobile hot meal distribution. Do you think you can handle it?"

"I'll take care of it," I told him with more confidence than I had. The goal was to distribute 100 lunches and dinners every day. That didn't seem like a lot, but considering we wanted each meal to be hot and we only had one small van to do it from, this was going to be a challenge.

The next morning when our van was loaded and we were heading out, I wondered for the first time how we would do it. I knew where we were going, but what was I actually supposed to do.

We pulled up to the first house in the small neighborhood closest to the dock. The homes themselves looked beautiful. They were two-story, brightly painted homes with little accents that made it look expensive. But in front of the home was a pile of trash. Most of it was expensive furniture and stainless steel appliances.

Not even sure if anyone was there, I took one of the warm plates with me to the front door. Knocking, I waited for a while for someone to answer. No one did.

Giving up, I went to the next house. Knocking had the same result. I was beginning to wonder if anyone would be home anywhere. That all changed after I knocked on the third door. A dirt-covered little boy answered it.

"Can I help you?" the 10-year-old asked.

"Yes, hi there. We're giving out free hot meals and I was wondering if you wanted one?"

The boy looked up at me doe-eyed then yelled, "Mom!"

Still standing in the doorway, the boy stared at me until a woman arrived behind him.

"Yes? Can I help you?" the almost as dirty woman said to me.

"Hi. We've been working from the docks giving out hot meals. Moving forward we will be delivering them to a few areas. I was wondering if you wanted one."

The woman's mouth dropped open stunned.

"Umm, yes, please. Can I get one for my kids as well?"

"Of course. And we'll be bringing dinner. Just let us know you'll be here and we'll put you on our list."

The woman's shocked face melted into tears. "Thank you!" She said dropping her steely mask. "You don't know how much it means to us."

She was right. I didn't, but I was slowly learning.

On the first day, all of my meetings were similar. Dirty people were answering the door with gratitude and a gleam of hope in their eyes. It was the most fulfilling experience of my life. Which is why, when I was handing out the last of the dinners, I didn't expect to knock on a door and hear,

"Jules?"

I couldn't speak. He was as good looking as the day I saw him at the airport. He was shirtless with gloves on and he was carrying a hammer. The sight of him took my breath away.

"Reed."

"Jules, what are you doing here?"

"I am distributing hot meals to the residence. Did you want one?" I asked trying to steady myself.

"Ahh… sure," he said accepting the plate. "That's not what I meant, though. I meant, what are you doing on the island?"

"I'm volunteering."

"Since when?"

"For about a week and a half now."

Reed stared at me and then shook his head trying to understand what was going on.

"Where's Laine?" he asked next.

"Oh. Yeah, Laine. We're not together."

"What happened?" Reed asked with genuine concern.

"It's a long story which I would like to tell you. Do you think we could get together sometime? I would love to catch up."

"Yeah, of course. How about tonight?"

"Tonight?"

"Yeah. Where are you staying?" Reed asked.

"I'm staying with the group I'm volunteering with. It's not far from the dock at the Hilton Resort."

"Do you think you can get to Stuart's? It's a conch salad stand in town. They aren't open for business. It's just where a few of us go when we need to stretch our legs."

"Sure. What time?"

"How about nine?"

"I'll be there," I told him.

"Great. I look forward to it," he said with a smile.

"Me too," I said before turning around and walking away.

When I got to the van I looked back. He was still watching me. It made my skin tingle.

Delivering the last of the meals, we headed back to the base station and made our way home for the night. Taking a shower was impossible but I did get in the front of the line for a bath.

Boiling the water on the stove, I poured it into the tub. Getting in it felt incredible. We didn't have much, so this little bit of indulgence made me feel like a million dollars.

It wasn't until after I got out and dried off that I remembered all of the things I would have to tell Reed. I couldn't imagine him responding well. I had lied to him so that Laine could manipulate him. There was no version of the story where I came out looking good.

Leaving our cottage, I found the streets dark. The town had yet to get electricity. At night we relied on the moon. That night was a full moon making the walk easier. And making my way to where I was told Stuart's was, I entered a square with dozens of people meandering around.

I had never imagined a place like this while I was hunkered down at the charity's rental cottage. From what had happened at the docks on the first day, and from all of the tired, dirty faces I ran into delivering food, I hadn't imagined that this was also possible.

There was a campfire in the middle of the parking lot and folks were gathered around it. Beyond that, they were laughing and smiling. It was actually kind of nice. Who would have guessed the capacity of the human spirit to find each other?

"Jules!" Reed's familiar voice called from behind me.

I turned seeing him. He was no longer sweaty and dirty. He had cleaned up nicely. In fact, he had already been in great shape, but now his clothes hung on him even better. I swallowed when I saw him. I again felt like a nervous college girl.

"Reed, hey," I told him before we awkwardly went in for a greeting. Offering my hand, he leaned in for a kiss on the cheek. We eventually settled on a hug.

"So, what are you doing here?" he asked after we found a spot near the fire and sat.

"Well, after I got back to California, I kept thinking about you down here. And, after I saw the pictures from the news, I knew I had to come down and do what I could to help."

"That's so good of you," he said clearly moved. "We need the help. Things have been rough."

"You know, this entire time I haven't been able to stop thinking about Thelma with the mangos," I said hoping the memory would make Reed smile. It didn't. It caused him to look away.

"Yeah, Thelma. She's recovering."

"What happened?" I asked concerned.

"The hurricane wasn't good to her. We think her parents might have drowned while they were holding her baby."

"Oh my god!" I exclaimed heartbroken.

"There's lots of tragedy. But, also there's hope. Groups like yours have really helped. That first day we felt so alone. But when the international generosity kicked in, it made all of the difference in the world. We're incredibly grateful," he said with a smile.

"So, what about you?" he asked me changing the topic. "You said that you and Laine are no longer together. What happened?"

This was it. This moment was going to decide everything about our relationship moving forward. My heart thumped knowing that I couldn't put it off any longer.

"I have a confession to make."

"What's that?"

"A lot of what I told you about Laine and me wasn't true."

"What do you mean? How much of it?"

"Most of it?"

Reed, who had been leaning toward me, shifted back. I continued.

"We weren't engaged. In fact, when I arrived on the island was only the second time I had seen him since college."

"Wait, I don't understand."

"He paid me a lot of money to pretend to be his fiancé. But I didn't know it was you who I would be pretending for. He just told me it was a friend. I really needed the money so I agreed. I never suspected how things would end up."

Reed stared at me shocked. "So, you're telling me that from the moment we met, you've been lying to me?"

"No. Not quite. Everything I told you about my life outside of Laine was true. And, what I said about the way he and I met was also what happened. Thanks for the tip, by the way. It turns out that he had been manipulating me from the moment I joined his temp agency. I think it was his plan to make me more and more desperate for money until I would have no choice but leap at his offer. The man's a psychopath."

"Laine isn't a psychopath," Reed said unexpectedly. "He's a lot of bad things and he's made a lot of poor decisions about how to treat people, but he's not a psychopath."

"Okay, well, I'm not sure how you can defend him considering how he manipulated us both."

"I'm not defending him. I'm just pointing out that psychopaths don't have sympathy or empathy. As misguided as he might be, I know he has both."

"Okay. But that doesn't excuse him for what he did."

"It doesn't," Reed agreed. "Just like how the money you got, doesn't excuse you."

Hearing him made my heart break. He was right. I couldn't argue against it.

"I agree. Maybe that has a lot to do with why I'm here. Maybe I'm trying to make amends. Maybe I'm trying to rescue what it was that we had and see if we have a future?"

"Oh," Reed said surprised.

"Do you think that's possible, Reed? Do you think the two of us could have a future together?" I asked vulnerably.

Chapter 6

Laine

If there was one thing I was sure of after leaving Bimini, it was that that self-righteous son-of-bitch was out of my mind for good. I was done with him. I mean, who the hell did he think he was?

He said that I don't know what love is? How about, he has no idea what family is? Or loyalty. I put my heart in my hands for him and he spat on it. I was done with him. There were 3 billion other people in the world and there was no way on earth that I was going to give another thought to him.

In fact, ever since I walked away from Jules, I've been living life like it was supposed to be lived. I left backwoods Florida for my penthouse in New York City. The great thing about my building is that there is always something to do.

Only the richest people in the world could afford to live where I live and for most of them, it is their second or third home… in New York. Our building is simply there so that we can play. Tonight I'm on my way down to Blaze's place.

Blaze is an interesting character. He was a star running back in the NFL. His end zone dances made him famous, but it was his post-football investments that made him rich.

Rumor is that he was on some type of undetectable performance enhancer that he later patented. Forming a biotech company around it, it now earns 2 billion a year. I don't invest in biotech but his company's stock is through the roof on word that he is working on something that will change life as we know it.

Yeah, right. After you buy that, I have a bridge in Brooklyn I'd like to sell you. None of his marketing bullshit matters tonight, though. Tonight, he's just a man who knows how to throw incredible parties. And judging from the selection of women, I'm about to have a lot of fun.

"What do you do?" a woman at the bar asked me in a thick Eastern European accent.

"I buy and sell companies. What do you do for fun?" I asked her.

"Men who like to buy and sell companies," she said pushing her rail-thin model body onto mine.

"Laine!" I heard someone yell at me over the music. "You made it?"

Turning around I spotted the man of the hour, Blaze himself. His tailored suit hugged his built form like a glove. That man was good looking. He was the only one in here that gave me any competition.

"Blaze? How are you? Great party. I was just getting to know," I turned back to the woman. "I'm sorry, what was your name?"

"Svetlana," she said purringly.

"I was just getting to know Svetlana, here."

"Yeah, of course," he said with a smile.

Grabbing my arm, he pulled me aside. "Trust me, you do not want that one. A little-used up, if you know what I mean."

"Good to know," I said before following him away.

"So, how was your trip? Did you land your deal?" he asked me casually.

Although he didn't know, he was asking about Reed. I had been discussing it with him over the past few months while leaving out the details. Men at our level are used to that. Sometimes we need advice and who better to ask but our wildly successful friends. The problem is that if the deal is good enough, they would run over their mother to steal it from you. So, all of the details were always left out.

"That's a no on the deal. In fact, it exploded in my face."

"Hopefully not literally," Blaze said grabbing my face and playfully examining it.

"Not literally, but close."

"Damn. That's too bad. What happened, if you don't mind me asking?"

"It was the hurricane," I told him honestly.

"The one that just hit Florida?"

"Yeah."

"Was it a land deal?"

"I was trying to obtain some property," I said thinking of Reed's incredible ass.

"Oh, that's too bad."

"Tell me about it."

"So, the deal's dead?"

"It's dead. Stone cold dead."

"That sucks. You were excited about it."

"I was. I was too excited."

"You made it sound like it was the deal of a lifetime." Blaze chuckled. "You sounded like one of those movie jewel thieves. This was your one big score where if you made it, you'd be able to give up the criminal life and retire on a beautiful island somewhere."

"Did I?" I said not realizing that I had.

"Yeah. I really had never seen you so excited about a deal. It was nice. You sure there's no way you can resurrect it? I mean, if the deal is as good as you made it seem, it might be worth trying."

"No, I think this one is done."

"Like I said, it's too bad. Maybe I can introduce you to a few ladies who might help you to forget about it."

"Blaze, you always know the perfect gift," I told him with a smile.

Crossing the large penthouse, the sea of beautiful people parted as we approached. We were their kings. The women hoped that one of us would choose them for the night, and the guys… hell, they probably wanted the same thing.

Blaze led me to the balcony bar which overlooked Central Park. Admiring the view were two equally lovely women skimpily dressed in loosely fitting white satin. The dresses would be easy to remove. I considered fucking one of them on the balcony so that everyone inside could see how fucking was supposed to be done. Instead, I allowed Blaze to show me the sights.

"Laine, this is Kaitlyn, and Katia," Blaze said before the girls stepped closer to me.

"Hello. Wait, are you two sisters?" I asked them.

"We're twins," they said in unison and with identical Swedish accents.

"The girls are models. And I said to them, "You know who might be able to put you in contact with the right people? My friend, Laine. Because Laine knows everyone." Laine, do you know the right people for them?"

I looked the two women up and down. They were gorgeous. I could imagine them gracing every runway from New York to Milan. And Blaze was right. I did know everyone.

"Yeah. Why don't you girls call the Wilhelmina Agency. Hammond will answer the call. Tell him that Laine Toros told you to call and that you should speak to Gia. They know me there. They trust my eye. And when you go in, be ready."

"Are you serious?" Kaitlyn said. "Is he serious?" she turned asking Blaze.

"I told you, my friend Laine knows everyone. That's his superpower."

"My superpower is my five billion dollar investment portfolio. But, knowing everybody is good too," I said with my most charming smile.

"Did you say five billion dollars?" Katia said to me before sliding beside me and putting her hand on my ass.

"Yeah. And don't be jealous, Blaze. Has your company grossed a billion yet?" I asked teeing Blaze up.

"You're working on old numbers, my friend. It looks like this year we'll make two."

"Two billion?" Kaitlyn asked wrapping her arm around Blaze.

"Yeah. Do you ladies invest?" Blaze asked them.

They looked at each other and giggled.

"Maybe we can go somewhere a little more private and talk about it," Blaze suggested to their delight.

Blazed gave me a pleased look as the two sisters latched onto us and our host led us away. It wasn't a long walk to the master bedroom. After Blaze closed the door, the volume of the party music receded into the background.

I looked around to see the type of space I was dealing with. The place was big. The bed was huge. The two of us could fuck either woman and never have to worry about crossing swords.

"So, are you ladies really twins?" Blaze asked charmingly.

"Uh-huh," Kaitlyn replied.

"We're identical," Katia added.

"I don't believe you. Laine, do you believe them?" Blaze said inviting me to sit on the bed.

"I don't know. I'm going to need to see some proof," I said joining him.

The two girls looked at each other and giggled. With blushing smiles, they stood in front of us. Each removing the spaghetti straps from their shoulders, their dresses dropped in unison. They stood before us completely naked and their bodies were perfect.

Katia looked me in the eyes with burning lust. Approaching me, she straddled my groin pressing her hardened nipples against my silk shirt. Kneeling up, she rubbed her body against mine. Returning her pussy to my groin, she leaned in and kissed my lips.

That was when it happened. Feeling her soft lips against mine, my mind flashed to the last person I had kissed, Reed. Even now with every man's greatest fantasy snake charming my cock, he was invading my thoughts. And once he got in, he refused to leave.

My mind flashed onto the heat between him and me the first time I leaned into him. I thought about how I took his tongue into my mouth. I thought about lightly tugging his hair.

That must have gotten my cock brick-hard because that was when Katia went wild. Unbuttoning my shirt, she kissed down my neck onto my chest. Flicking my nipple with her tongue, she reached down unbuttoning my pants. When I had done that to Reed, my next move was to suck his cock. God damn did he have a great cock. How could he have such a great cock?

It was as Katia kissed my taught stomach that I did it. I committed the greatest sin a guy could commit. I reached down, slipped my hand under her chin and guided her eyes back up to mine.

"I want to see the two of you fuck Blaze," I told her to Blaze's surprise.

"Okay," she said happy to please me.

Blaze, who was as undressed as I was, looked over at me delighted. This wasn't the first time we had had women together. I knew him. He was a showman. At this point, he was probably more turned on by me watching than yet another perfect feminine form.

Katia joined her twin on top of Blaze and the two of them went to work. Kaitlyn wrapped her hands around Blaze's cock and traced the tip of her pointy tongue around the rim of his head. I had to admit, Blaze had a nice one. It wasn't as long as mine, but it was a little thicker.

Katia, meanwhile, went for his lips and laid her small body on the chest of the much taller man.

Blaze certainly was the performer. Wasting no time, he pulled Kaitlyn onto his cock. Leaning forward, she pressed on her sister as support while climbing on. She was going to ease onto him slowly, but Blaze would have none of it. He latched onto her waist and thrust his hips. She squealed with painful pleasure. When her muscles relaxed and her neck became rubber, she rode him like a bucking bronco.

Letting go of her sister, she sat up pushing her hands through her lush hair. Moaning with her eyes closed, she was clearly in another world. It had to be his thickness that was driving her wild. She was sprinting to orgasm. Gripping her hair like a madwoman, her moans became screeches before her hands flung forward again resting her hands on her sisters' lower back for support.

Lifting her hips but not removing Blaze completely, she froze. Her body had entered the clench that preceded spasm. When the damn broke, it was like she was having a seizure. She would relax and then spasm again. And when Blaze became tired of waiting for the fucking to resume, he brushed her aside, positioned Katia face down over Kaitlyn's quivering body and moved behind her.

That was when I pulled up my pants and got up. As Blaze wrapped his ex-football player hands around Katia's tiny waist and pushed himself into her, I was buttoning my shirt. I smiled watching the scene when I realized that those girls didn't know what they had gotten themselves into. Kaitlyn was still quivering on the bed when her sister laid her head on Kaitlyn's breasts. The women clung to each other for dear life. They were what true pleasure looked like, and the sight made me want that for myself.

Slipping out of the room, I reentered the sea of beautiful people. Looking around, each person was better looking than the next. Like at every other party, I knew that I could have any one of them, the guys included. But did I want that?

Again I was under the spell of that self-righteous bastard, but this time I had just left him. I had long accepted that he was my drug. One hit of him would last me almost a year. But this time, it had barely been two weeks.

What the hell was happening to me? Reed made me feel bad about myself. He made me question my life choices. And this time he questioned my ability to love.

He was not good for me. Yet, once again, I was stuck on him.

In the middle of every man's fantasy, I could only think of him. Walking through a sea of beauties, all I wanted was him. And with the time and money to go anywhere in the world, the only place I wanted to be was in his arms feeling his lips against mine one more time.

When I told him that I loved him, I had been completely sure of it. Later I thought that I might have been saying it because of the drama of the approaching storm. But here I was miles away and safe and sound, yet what I said then, I can say now. I love him and I am in love with him.

"God damn it, I'm in love with Reed," I said with realization.

"What?" a cute girl beside me asked.

I looked at her. She was staring back at me with a blush. Everything about her told me that I could have her if I wanted. But I didn't. I only had eyes for one person, and it fucking sucked. No, seriously, what the hell was wrong with me?

I left the party without saying another word. I could feel everyone's eyes on me as I left. I didn't care. There was only one person whose attention I wanted and he was on an island a thousand miles away. I needed to figure out how to get back to him. I was willing to move heaven and earth to make that happen.

The first thing I did when I was again alone in my suite was to turn on the news. Ever since arriving home, I had refused to do it. The coverage of the hurricane was everywhere. I didn't want to hear anything about it. Now I wanted to hear everything.

Unbuttoning my sleeves and rolling them up, I crossed the room to my office and opened my laptop. Typing in 'Hurricane Betty', I sat down and watched as the avalanche of results appeared before me.

By morning, I hadn't read all of it, but I had to have read most. I knew the death toll, the damage estimate, and which groups were already on the ground assisting. Deep diving the groups, I knew what type of relief they were offering, their pattern of delivery, and what they didn't do.

My man had implied that the island's recovery was important to him, so, from this point on, it was important to me, too. I was going to show him why having money was good. And once and for all, I would prove to him that I knew how to love him.

"Jamie, I want you to get the world's foremost expert on hurricane recovery on the phone," I told my assistant.

"Yes, sir. Would you happen to know who that is?" he asked.

"I can tell you it's not me, and I really doubt it's you. That's all I got."

"Yes, sir," he said running with my very helpful input.

To Jamie's continued credit, someone he described as the foremost expert, who spoke English, was on the phone with me within the hour.

"Tell me what Bimini needs. And, money is no object," I told him to his stunned surprise.

It took a week. Or, perhaps I should say that it *only* took a week. With his help, I was standing on the bow of a cargo ship so loaded with building supplies that we were close to taking on water.

Building supplies were the key. Everyone thinks about the essentials, food, water, housing, but that was just stage one of disaster relief. That was the keeping-people-from-dying stage. What Roberto helped me to understand was that those were the things that international relief organizations took care of. What every nation hit by a disaster always struggled with was the cost and availability of the materials necessary to return their lives to normal.

That was what I was bringing. Plywood, sheetrock, 2×4, that stuff you spray on the ceiling to make it look cheap, I had it all. On top of that, I had stoves, fridges, microwave ovens, and the rest.

If there was room for them, I would have brought them cars. Standing on the bow of the ship, I would have pointed at people saying, "You get a car. You get a car.

Everybody gets a car!" I would have gone full Oprah on their ass.

But, there wasn't enough space. And Roberto insisted that it wasn't what they needed. So, instead, I bought out every building supplies wholesaler in Florida and loaded it onto a rented cargo ship.

Pulling into the harbor, it was clear that everyone knew what was coming. They were cheering. Yes, someone may have radioed ahead and informed them of Christmas in July. We were going to have to get it to them somehow. This way, everyone who needed it came to get it for themselves and Reed got to see me greeted as the conquering hero. Everyone wins.

Another person who wins would be Reed, himself. Certainly, his little shack would have been damaged during the hurricane. Most of the island was underwater. Entire electrical systems had to be replaced. He needed supplies just like everyone else.

He was going to be on the dock and he was going to see that everyone was cheering for me. How could the cheers not show him how wrong he was about me? Of course it would. And finally I would have the upper hand in this relationship. Finally, he would be the one chasing after me.

The cheers didn't stop until long after we began giving out supplies. The entire time I stood just inside the cargo doors pointing out who would get the next load we sent out. Really, I was there to find Reed in the crowd.

There were thousands of people there. It took a while to find him. But when I did, I felt butterflies swarm my stomach. Staring down into his eyes, I knew that I was about to get what I had wanted for so long.

"Him," I said pointing at Reed as the next person to make their request.

Seeing one of my men run over to him with the request sheet, I smiled feeling really good about myself. I was his savior. It felt awesome. When he handed the sheet off, I made my way down to him. This was it. Finally! FINALLY, I would get what I had always deserved from him.

"Reed," I said greeting him.

"Laine, you came back," he said with zero emotion.

"Yeah. Of course. What was I going to do? Nothing?" I said with one of my best charming smiles.

"You are full of surprises," he said as if it were no big deal.

"Something wrong?" I asked him knowing that something was going on. Even with whatever had gone down between us, I was sensing a real lack of gratitude.

"No. Everything's great, I guess thanks to you," he said with a half-hearted smile.

I stared at him trying to figure him out. Giving up, I decided to just say it.

"Okay, the words you're saying are making me think that you're grateful. But, what's confusing me is the way you're saying it."

"What do you mean?" he asked flatly.

"I mean that… Okay, I'll admit it. I assumed you'd be here and when you saw this, you would be… I don't know, happier. I mean, isn't this what you wanted. Do you know what's on that ship and what's coming later? *Fifty million dollars'* worth of building supplies and goods."

I stopped talking allowing that number to set it.

"That's amazing, Laine. Thank you. Really, thank you."

Do you know how being seasick feels? That was how I felt now, because what I was experiencing wasn't lining up with what my eyes and ears were telling me.

"Okay, you're saying that, but I don't think you're really saying that."

"I don't know what you're talking about, Laine," he said being annoyingly Reed. "I don't know what to tell you. I've said thank you. Everyone here is very grateful for what you've done."

"Wait, do you think I give a shit about these people. Is that why you thought I did it? For their gratitude? No, Reed, I did this," I pointed to the ship, "I did this all for you. I spent fifty million dollars for you."

"What do you want me to say, Laine? I said thank you. What else is there for me to say?" he asked as if the man was dead inside.

"What do I want you to say? More than fucking this! Jesus Christ, Reed, what more do you want from me? You want my fuckin' blood? Take it! What more can I give you? Tell me, Reed, what more can I fuckin' give you?"

"Nothing, Laine. There's nothing more you can give me. This is enough, Laine. You've done enough," he said as if someone had drowned his cat on his birthday.

"Ahhhh!" I screamed having had enough.

"This was not the way this was supposed to go!" I informed him.

"How was this supposed to go?"

"Fuck you!" I told him and then stormed my way through the crowd.

I was so furious that I had no idea what to do with myself. I was ready to walk forever. I was considering having my men collect everything back, packing it onto the ship and heading home. I was just about to do it, too, when I saw another familiar face. She was directly in front of me.

"Jules?" I said coming to an abrupt stop.

She opened her mouth to speak when I cut her off saying what was clearly on both of our minds.

"What the fuck is wrong with him? Seriously, what the FUCK… is wrong… with him." I pointed at the ship again. "Fifty million dollars. FIFTY MILLION! WHAT THE FUCK IS WRONG WITH HIM?"

With the blood vessels in my brain feeling like they were about to burst, I stared at her waiting for her to speak. She was giving me the same dead stare that Reed had given me moments before. Was there some type of zombie virus on the island that I didn't know about? There couldn't be because earlier people were practically chanting my name.

No, it was just these two. Something was up. And, as I thought about it, what the hell was Jules doing here? I was about to ask her that when the mute spoke.

"Hello, Laine," she said calmly.

That sobered me a bit. "What? Didn't I say hello?"

She continued staring at me. That's when I remembered how I had left things with her. The last time I was with her, she had just figured out that I had been behind getting her fired.

"Did you get your check?" I asked knowing that she did but deciding that it would be a good reminder of stuff.

"I did. Thank you," she said as flatly as Reed had.

"Jules, something tells me that you have a few things you want to say to me. I'll let you say whatever you need to. Just answer one question for me first."

"And, what's that?" she asked.

"What the fuck is wrong with Reed?" I asked her as sincerely as I could.

"He doesn't love you."

"What?"

"He doesn't love you," she repeated confusing me further about what was going on.

"What do you mean he doesn't love me?"

"You think that he should respond in some certain way because you two have some type of history together. But, he doesn't feel anything for you anymore."

"He doesn't feel anything for me anymore?" I asked feeling my world spin.

"He doesn't."

"How do know that?"

"Because he told me."

"He told you that?"

"Yep."

"So then, I guess he loves you," I said starting to see through her plan.

"Nope. He doesn't love me either."

"He doesn't love you? What exactly did you do?" I asked now incredibly confused.

"I helped you trick him, and I had lied to him from the moment I stepped off the plane."

"Oh, that," I said seeing the logic.

"Yeah that. Thanks for the money, by the way. It helped."

I gave her the eye not sure how to take that. "You know, you could have backed out at any time."

"I know. I made my bed, just like you did. And like you, now I'm lying in it."

"Soooo, things between us are good?"

"They're good," she said emotionlessly.

"Okay. By the way, how do you know how he feels about me?"

"I know because he told me. We're friends."

"You two are friends?"

"I'd like to call us that. I'd hope he would say the same."

I nodded my head piecing everything together. "So, you're saying that I fucked things up."

"You fucked things up," she confirmed.

"And, no matter what I do, including this, I won't be able to make things better?"

"That is the impression I got."

"Well, that sucks," I said to her now as calm as she was.

"That sucks," she empathized.

I would like to say that I accepted my circumstances like a man. I would like to say that I embraced my new reality with a stiff upper lip. But I didn't. Staring at Jules as she stared back, I had to swallow. It wasn't long before my eyes started to burn. My chest hurt so badly. And feeling a tickle in my nose I figured out what was happening.

I didn't want to do this. I wanted to hold myself together. I looked away trying to gather myself. But losing the safe haven of Jules's eyes, things only got worse. I tried to take a deep inhale and I whimpered.

Once the tears started, they didn't stop. I felt so much pain. My body shook with despair. Standing on the dock surrounded by judging faces, I wailed. I didn't care because at that moment it had hit me. As long as I had had Reed in my life, I had had someone. But, here, and for the first time, I was alone. Completely and utterly alone.

I thought I was going to stand there crying forever. I didn't. And the only reason for that was Jules. Despite everything I had done, she walked up to me and wrapped her arms around me. She held me as I cried, and for that, I was eternally grateful.

"What do I do now?" I asked her once the tears slowed and my body stopped shaking.

"I don't know," she said to me sounding sincere. "What you did here, though, it really was a good thing."

"What does that even mean?" I asked her not seeing the point to anything.

Jules pulled away, grabbed my shoulders and looked me in the eyes. "It means that you really helped a lot of people."

"Okay."

"No. Listen to me. You changed a lot of people's lives here today."

I shook my head telling her how little what she said meant to me. I mean, I could see she was trying to help. But really, what did any of what she said mean?

"I think I know what you should do," she said to me as I wiped my eyes.

"What's that?"

"You should stick around."

"Why?"

"To see the effects your generosity had on these people's lives."

I shook my head about to express how little such things meant to me.

"Before you say no, ask yourself what else you have to do right now."

I looked at the most naïve person on the planet unsure of what to say. I ran a billion-dollar company. There were a billion things that demanded my attention, and all of them were more important than wasting my time here.

"Jules…"

"Just stay. Don't think about it, just stay. You obviously blocked off some time to be here, so be here. But, I mean, like, BE here. Don't just obsess about Reed, or sit on your ship. Be here."

"What makes you think I'd obsess about Reed?"

"Because I obsessed about Reed after he told me what he had. And you've been in love with him a lot longer than I have. Look, think of this as a vacation."

"Jules, I worry that you don't know what a vacation is."

Jules laughed. "I know what a vacation is. I remember our fake trip to Paris."

It was my turn to laugh. "Yes, my favorite part was when we pretend-went to the Eiffel Tower."

"Where you proposed?" Jules said playfully taking my hands in hers.

"You remember."

"How could I forget the greatest imaginary vacation of my life?"

Staring at Jules I couldn't help but chuckle. I didn't know if she was right or not, or if she had a point or not. What I did know was that anywhere I were to go wouldn't have her in it. And, as little as I knew about her, I knew that she and I had once shared an experience that meant a lot to me. She was the closest thing I had left to a friend.

"Okay. I'll stay. I still don't see the point, though."

"There's no point. It's just a choice. But, I think it will be a good choice for you. Certainly, it's been a good choice for me."

Jules told me how to contact her and encouraged me to get ahold of her if I wanted to hang out or chat. I wasn't sure whether or not I would. Honestly, I wasn't even sure whether or not I would stay. I did, though. And for the first few days, I didn't leave the ship.

When I got tired of sulking like a toddler, I decided to find Jules. She had told me that her team met every morning at a nearby dock. So, getting up early and walking over, I was there when she arrived.

"Laine!" She said appearing to be in a good mood. "Everyone, this is Laine Toros. He's the one who brought all of the building supplies."

"Is this him?" a guy with a speckled beard and kind eyes said.

"That's him," Jules told him with a smile.

"Whitfield Cooper," he said offering me his hand. "I'm the director of the meals program here. I have to say, what you did probably saved a few lives."

"Okay," I told him pretty sure that wasn't the case.

"You don't believe me," he asked reading my obvious skepticism.

"Hey, Jules, why don't you take him on your afternoon run. I think he'll get a kick out of seeing how his donations are being used."

"You got it, Chief," Jules told him. "What do you say, Laine, wanna join me?"

"What would I have to do?"

"Listen to these lame asses drone on," she said playfully referring to the two young guys standing behind her.

"You know you like it," the heavier set one replied.

"I do. I'll admit it. They might not know what they're talking about, but they say it with such passion," Jules told me with a playful smile.

"Don't know what we're talking about? Everything I say is correct. You can't name me one thing I said that wasn't."

Jules looked at me as if she and I had an inside joke. "I would make him a list but humans only live to be a hundred?"

"Yeah, right. You know I'm right. You're just mad you didn't think of these things first," the round guy said ready to argue about it forever.

"What do you say, Laine, you think you could stand listening to them?"

"I think I'll be fine," I told her kind of looking forward to being around normal people again. Billionaires and models were great and all, but conversations with them could get pretty boring.

Standing aside, I watched as the three of them helped cook lunch, put it on plates, and then loaded the van.

"Sit back here with me," Jules said as I made a move to open the front passenger door.

Giving it a moment of thought, I relented. Sliding onto the second row of seats in the tiny van, I remembered the last time Jules and I had been so close. It was the last night that the three of us were together. The flash of melancholy across her face told me that she had the same thought. I definitely missed having Reed in my life. But, I was now willing to accept the world I had created for myself.

"See all of that sheetrock on the lawn?" Jules said pointing out the pile at the first house we stopped at. "That's because of you."

Jules got out of the van and delivered three plates of food to someone who opened the door without her knocking.

"And, do you see that?" she asked when stopping at the next home. She said the same thing when we stopped at the third and the forth.

"I get it. I get it. Yes, I see. All of the homes are using the supplies. Everyone is very grateful," I told her.

Jules stared at me not loving my attitude. I wasn't sure what she was expecting from me. She was pointing it out, and I saw it. What more to the exchange was there than that?

"You know, I don't think you're getting it. That's my fault. Okay, I have a better idea. Let's get a few more of these plates delivered. Afterward, there's a place we'll go."

For the next hour, I sat in the van watching each time Jules got out, delivered the plates, and got back in. It got tedious. I didn't know how much more of this I could take. I was about to ask them to drop me off somewhere when Jules's mood shifted.

"Okay. We have two more plates to deliver and this time I want you to come with me when I do."

"You got it," I agreed sure that anything would be better than sitting in the back of a van in the Bahamas in the middle of summer.

"We're stopping here?" I asked her when the van again pulled over.

"Yeah, what's wrong?" She asked genuinely not knowing.

"Nothing. Carry on."

The reason I had asked was because most of the homes we had stopped at were quite nice apart from the garbage on the lawn. The one we had now stopped at probably wasn't that nice looking even during the best of times. It was a bit of a downgrade, if you know what I mean.

Grabbing two of the last few plates in the van, Jules led the way as I followed in her wake.

"I bet you don't know what sheetrock is used for," she said as we passed the bent back chain link fence and approached the door.

"I bet you're wrong," I told her knowing exactly what it was used for. My research had been thorough.

"Okay, but have you ever seen what a house looks like without it?"

She had me there. I had not. "Is that what this little trip is about?"

Jules made a clicking noise with her mouth and winked. With her hands full, she couldn't make the accompanying finger guns, but clearly, she wanted to.

A woman opened the door as soon as we approached greeting us with a big smile.

"Heeeey, Jules, how are you today?"

"Good, good. This is Laine. He's with the team that brought the building supplies. Do you mind if I show him around your place? I want to give him a feel for how it's being used."

"Of course," she said happily.

The woman was not much older than Jules or I, and with her overly gracious demeanor, she reminded me of someone, though I couldn't think of who.

"Come in, please," she said taking the plates from Jules and guiding us in.

The place was small and pretty barren.

"After the flooding, we had to throw everything out," the woman explained seeming to make an excuse for her home's emptiness. "Anything made of wood warped. And anything that wasn't dried right away got moldy and had to be thrown out as well."

Jules added, "Most of the homes had to get all of their walls cut open so that the water between the sheetrock and the outer wall could dry. Otherwise, mold develops and it could enter your lungs and make you sick."

The woman spoke again. "And with a kid in the house, I had to think about his health. I was thinking about not cutting the walls open because, you know, where am I going to find the money to repair it? But, the kid, so…," she said with a shrug.

"Of course," I told her. "Do you mind if I look around?"

"No, go ahead. I think my son's back there somewhere. Just ignore him if he bothers you."

Yeah, she definitely reminded me of someone. That was part of the reason I asked to walk around by myself. There was something uncomfortable about her. There was something uncomfortable about all of this. But clearly, Jules was trying to make some sort of point. I thought that I would at least make an attempt to see it.

The place wasn't big so it didn't take me very long to see everything in the living room. I got it. The woman was living with the electrical plugs and pipes exposed. It wasn't great. The sheetrock would solve that. It helped.

Going down the short hallway I approached one of the two bedroom doors. Entering the one on the right I found two things, a bed and a poster on the wall. Like everywhere else, the walls were missing sheetrock. But in spite of that, there was a poster still wrapped in its original plastic that was tacked onto the wall. More than that, the poster was of my car. I mean, not mine specifically, but my year, model, and color.

"I'm going to get that car when I grow up," I heard a kid's voice say.

I turned spotting a kid sitting quietly in the corner of the room. He wasn't playing or doing anything. The 9-year-old boy was just sitting with his back against the corner of the wall.

"It's a nice car," I told him. "I actually own one of them."

"You do?" The boy said suddenly perking up.

"I do. That color and everything."

"That's so cool!"

"Yeah, it is," I said with a smile. "I'm Laine. What's your name?" I asked always glad to meet a fellow car enthusiast.

"Damian," he said extending his hand.

"Nice to meet you, Damian. So, you wanna get that car, do you?"

"Yeah. It cost $130,000."

"Yes it does," I said with a chuckle.

"How could you afford $130,000? You rich or something?"

I nodded. "Something like that. So, were you in here during the hurricane?"

"No. I was at the shelter. Do you know Brian?"

"Who's Brian?"

"He's my best friend. I haven't heard from him since the hurricane. I was hoping you saw him."

"I'm sorry, I haven't. Was he in a different shelter than you?"

Damian shrugged his shoulders. "Tell you what, I'll ask around. I know a few people. When we find him, I'll let him know you're looking for him. Okay?"

"Okay," Damian said disappointed.

"Don't worry, I'll find him," I said deciding what I would do for the rest of the day. "Anyway, it was good to meet you. And, great taste in cars," I said with a smile.

"Thank you," he said quickly returning to the state I had found him in.

It was as I took a final look around his room that it all hit me. I knew why the woman felt familiar. I knew why this place unnerved me. It was set up exactly like the tiny house I lived in after my father took off.

The woman had the same overly gracious demeanor my mother had when people came around offering handouts, and this place was literally nothing more than beds and floor. Hell, the boy had a poster of a car on the wall of my actual car. This kid was me.

Realizing it, I wanted out of there as quickly as possible. I couldn't guess whether Jules knew about the similarities. But, I suddenly hated everything about this little detour.

"You ready to go?" I asked her when I found Jules in the hollowed-out kitchen.

"Yeah, sure," she said breaking away from her conversation with the woman.

I led the group out the front door and was about to sprint to the van when the woman stopped me.

"Did my son ask you about his friend Brian?"

"Yeah," I said forced to turn back around.

"Did he ask you to look for him?"

"No, but I told him I would."

"You don't have to," she said in a hushed tone.

"No, that's fine. I'll ask around."

"I meant, you don't have to because we know where he is. He died during the hurricane. It's just my son and me and I don't have the heart to tell him his best friend's gone. He's been through so much already."

Hearing her, I lost my breath. "He lost his best friend because of the hurricane?" I asked her relating to this family way too much.

"Yeah," she said giving me a glimpse of the sadness she hid inside.

"We should go," I said feeling too much come to the surface.

I turned and began down the walkway when I quickly turned back. "Go to the dock and ask for a man by the name of Roberto. Tell him I sent you and he will set you up with a full set for your kitchen. Fridge, stove, oven, all that."

"Are you serious?" the woman asked.

"Yeah. No, you know what? I'll tell him. I'll have someone deliver them to you."

"Oh, thank you so much!"

I was about to turn and leave again when I said, "And, I'll… ah, have someone come down and help you with the sheetrock and stuff."

"Really?" she asked elated. "Thank you so much," she said starting to cry.

"Yeah. Don't worry about it," I told her doing everything I could to fight off the emotions. "Let's go, Jules," I said with my thoughts tumbling and my stomach churning.

Chapter 7

Reed

There is nothing good about the destruction and devastation that the hurricane brought. I've lost friends and my home. People like Thelma and I may never recover. But there are moments of respite.

Showing up to get breakfast at 7 a.m. with your crew was one of those moments. It's in moments like those when the island feels like one big community. Everyone has one purpose, to help bring back a sense of normalcy. All of our shared experiences during the hurricane bonds us together. There isn't anyone that we can't turn to in moments of despair. And in spite of everything, moments like this are what fill me with hope, not just for tomorrow but for humanity as a whole.

"I've been told that there's a new crew helping with finishing work," Julian said snatching me from my thoughts.

"Really? That's great," I told him glad to see that others have begun to pitch in.

"Yeah. They don't seem to have an organized schedule. So, I'm going to send you to house #4 in the 227 block. If that crew is already there, then move onto house #9. I told Ms. Miller that you could be stopping by today with your crew."

"Gotcha. By the way, who's the other crew? Are they local?"

"It's a mix, I think. You know the organization giving away the building supplies?"

"Yeah," I admitted hesitantly.

"The crew is associated with them. I think some of the locals might be getting paid. So, if you want to switch teams, feel free. I know you lost your home. Eventually, you're going to need to start earning some money. The free shelter and food won't last forever."

"Don't worry, I'll be here for as long as anyone needs me," I reassured him.

"I appreciate that. We all do. I hope you know that. But eventually, life is going to return to normal here. I just don't want you caught unprepared."

I smiled acknowledging his concern. It was nice that Julian was looking out for me. But there were a lot of other people who needed more help than I did right now.

Finishing up breakfast, the crew and I hopped into the truck and headed to our assignment. When we arrived we saw that there was already a truck parked out front. I could hear hammering coming from within. The other crew was already there. I was about to redirect the guys to the next location when I decided to go in. I had heard Julian's warning and there was no harm in introducing myself.

Getting out, I approached the open front door and peered in.

"Hello?" I said not wanting to intrude.

"Hi," someone said before slipping past me to head to the other truck.

I was thinking about chasing after him when I instead went inside and took a look around. Mine was a crew of three people. At least ten people were at work here. In the front room were two painters and in the bedrooms and baths were seven others.

This was amazing. With a crew this size, the entire house could be completed in days instead of the two weeks it took my crew. I was impressed and really curious to meet the site manager.

"Excuse me, hi," I said to one of the painters.

"Hey, how's it going," the young man said as he continued to work.

"I was wondering, who's your foreman."

"He said he was gunna be working in the backroom," the young man replied without ever looking at me.

Again crossing the hallway, I spotted the man who I had seen during my first round. He was dressed in overalls which were both covered in paint and laden with tools. He was in the process of attaching a sheet onto the wall so I waited until he was done before I spoke.

"Excuse me, someone told me you were the foreman," I said drawing his attention.

"Reed?" the man said surprised.

It took me a moment to recognize who it was. The clothing and locale had thrown me off. But when it hit me, it rocked me onto my heels and momentarily robbed me of speech.

"Laine? What... Why... You're the foreman?" I asked unable to make sense of what I was seeing.

"Yeah," Laine said standing up. "This is my crew, so I guess that makes me the foreman."

"What are you doing here?"

"Laying sheetrock. What are you doing here?"

"My crew was assigned to this house."

"Oh, did you guys want to work on this one?" Laine asked concern.

"No, no. You guys go ahead. We have somewhere else we can go. I just wanted to... Nevermind. I'll go."

I turned still stunned by what I had seeing.

"Actually, I was gonna come and find you. Can we talk?" Laine said following me into the living room.

I stopped and gave him my attention. "What is it?"

"Can we go somewhere private?"

I didn't like where his request seemed to be leading. Giving him a disapproving look, I told him, "I think here would be better."

Laine looked around at his crew who were all hard at work and relented.

"Okay. What I wanted to tell you is that I'm not going anywhere."

"What do you mean?"

"I mean, I'm not going anywhere. You can push me away. You can run and hide from your feelings like you have all of your life. But, I love you and I'm not going anywhere."

Laine hadn't said that quietly, so once he did, the painters stopped and the guys laying sheetrock came out of their rooms to stare at us. Feeling incredibly self-conscious, I wanted to escape.

"Okay, Laine. Noted," I said before turning to go.

He grabbed my arm holding me there.

"I'm serious, Reed. I'm not going anywhere. And every week I'm going to find you and remind you of this."

"Wait, what?"

"Every week, I'm going to find you, tell you that I love you, and remind you that I'm not going anywhere."

"Laine, why would you do that?"

"Because I really do love you, and I'm really not going anywhere."

"No, I mean, what makes you think I care?"

Laine let go of my arm and stared at me. "I don't know if you do, I guess. But, my feelings for you started the moment I met you that first week of college. And ever since, you've meant everything to me. Everything I do, I do thinking of you.

"What I've learned is that that's not going to change. It will continue independent of whether you care or not, whether you push me away or not. You're not going to be able to hide from us anymore. Because however you want to define our relationship, there is an "us". And my part of "us" loves you, and always will."

Stunned by what Laine had said, my eyes bounced from his to all of the others staring at us. Everyone was staring at us. His crew, my crew, they were all watching us with their mouths hanging open. I needed to get out of there. This time when I turned and walked off, Laine didn't try to stop me.

Pushing past my crew who now stood in the doorway, I lowered my head and headed to the truck. Getting in, my guys were slow to follow. When I was seated with the door closed and they weren't there, I reached over and hit the horn. That got them in the truck. Riding their awkward silence, Ryan started the truck and drove us away.

"That was weird, right?" I eventually said to the two guys beside me.

"I don't think it was weird," Ryan countered.

"I wish I had someone who loved me that much," Tommy replied never removing his focus from straight ahead.

That was the last time I brought it up with them. When we began work on house #9, things returned to normal. But that was when what Laine had said started rolling around in my mind.

"Did you know that Laine was still on the island?" I asked Jules when I saw her later that night.

"Yeah," she told me not even looking up from her meal.

"How?"

"I was the one who encouraged him to stay."

"Why would you do that?"

"He was in a dark place. I thought that being here would help him."

"Does that have anything to do with why he's working on houses? Was that your idea?"

"No, that was all him," she explained finally looking up.

"How did that happen?"

"I took him around to see how his supplies were changing lives and we stopped in to take a look at one of the homes. As we were leaving, he told the woman who lived there that he would send her some appliances and a crew to repair her house. The next day he showed up with both and was doing a lot of the work himself."

"I didn't know he knew how to do any of that," I told her surprised.

"I'm not sure he did," she said with a chuckle. "But he's been doing it every day for a few weeks now, and if you do anything enough, you get better."

"Do you think that this is another of his schemes?"

"No. Why?"

"Well, I saw him and he said some things that made me wonder."

"What did he say?" Jules asked very interested.

"It's kind of embarrassing."

"What did he say?"

"He said that he loved me and that every week he was going to find me and remind me of it."

"Wow!"

"Yeah. It was a bit much," I told her.

"No. I was thinking that it was really sweet."

"But, you know it's some kind of con, right?"

Jules looked away and then back at me. "The way he went about things was questionable, but he always did it for one purpose, to get you to love him. I guess this time he decided to take the direct route. The question is, how do you feel about him?"

"I told you how I feel. I feel nothing for him."

"Have you always felt nothing, or is this new?"

"I…" I began before thinking twice. "He did say something that made me think."

"What was that?"

"He said that I was hiding from my feelings for him and that I always had."

"Do you think that's true?" Jules asked laser-focused on our conversation.

I leaned back and crossed my arms uncomfortable with this topic.

"I think in the past I might have taken the easy way out of things. I mean, look at us back in college. I had the biggest crush on you... the biggest crush. Yet, why didn't I ever say something to you about it?

"And, yeah, there might have been a time when I had feelings for Laine. And those feelings might have existed for as long as he claims to have had feelings for me. But, instead of following him to New York, I came here and then barely kept in contact with him."

Jules, who was frozen as I spoke, returned to chewing once I finished. "Here's an interesting question. How different would your life have been if you would have said anything to either of us about how you felt?"

"I would guess a lot different," I told her sincerely.

"And, here's another question — and I haven't forgotten what he and I both did to you — but, is it possible that you could be using what we did as an excuse to not have to deal with your feelings? Since we are now both on the same island as you and available, could your anger at us be your new way of hiding?"

Mic drop. Wow! I did not see that one coming. I quickly changed the topic, but that was all I could think about for the rest of the week.

Could my anger at them be my new way of hiding from how I felt about the both of them? The sad thing was that I wouldn't put it past me. I've had a great life living on Bimini, but there's no denying that it hasn't been a complete life.

Who have I loved during the ten years I've been here? I've loved Jules, and as much as I would like to deny it, Laine. There was that one sexual encounter but no one else who I've loved.

On the other hand, how could I forgive the two of them for what they did to me? They lied to me and tricked me. They made me feel like a fool. And, for what reason? Jules did it for money. And, Laine… why? To rub his success in my face? To show me that he could have whatever he wanted? Honestly, I didn't know why he did it. And I wasn't sure I cared.

The following week was going to be the hardest since the hurricane. During the first week, we had recovered a lot of bodies. The Johnsons' and Thelma's baby were not among them. That meant that there wasn't a need to rush their funeral, and that celebrating their life could wait.

The wait was now over. This was their time. Instead of having individual funerals, the three were going to be memorialized at once. As my friends and my godchild, this was going to be rough. As her closest non-blood relative, I helped Thelma with all of the arrangements.

On the day of the funeral, I could barely hold myself together.

"I would like to be there for you," Jules told me. "I know that you might prefer to spend it with the family or that you might still be upset with me…"

"Yes," I said cutting her off. "I would love it if you could go with me," I confessed immediately reaching for her hand.

Hers was a big smile. When I saw tears forming in her eyes, I had to fight off my own.

"You're supposed to be helping me not to cry," I said with a tear-filled chuckle.

With Jules's hand planted firmly in mine, we entered the church making our way to the front row. Jules was there for me, and my job was to be there for Thelma who was handling it as well as anyone might expect.

I was so grateful that I had Jules there. Whatever she had done in the past, she had more than made up for it now. It was undeniable that she cared about me. Which is why I couldn't understand why, even now as she was being my rock, I couldn't get myself to feel the feelings I felt bubbling under the surface.

She had been right to point out that she was not only here on the island, but that she was available. What was it that refused to let me be happy?

Sitting at his memorial I was reminded of one of the many times I had spoken to Mr. Johnson about Jules. He had said to me that, "Sometimes you just gotta go for it. You can't sit back waiting for things to come to you."

He had said it to encourage me to look her up. That was way beyond something I could ever get myself to do. I guess he was wrong because, in the end, I didn't have to. Here I was walking out of his memorial hand in hand with her, and it was all thanks too…

"Laine?" I coughed seeing him sitting in front of me in the last pew.

"I'm sorry for your loss," he said tightening his lips with genuine empathy.

"Thank you," I told him confused by what he was doing there but not willing to stick around to ask.

Later at the wake, I spotted Laine again. He was having a long conversation with a local woman. This was not like him. The Laine I knew would never be caught dead at a place like this. And, someone like the woman he was speaking to would never be worthy of his time.

"How do you know Laine?" I later asked the woman.

"He and his men did the repairs on my house. He's such a lovely guy. Did you know that he paid for all of it? Everything. He even replaced my fridge. He's like an angel."

"An angel who doesn't have a problem taking credit," I said feeling a little cynical.

"What do you mean?" the woman asked.

"I mean it's great that he did it, but he also made sure that he got credit for it."

"Oh no," she said disturbed that I would suggest such a thing. "I didn't know until a neighbor told me who he was. He doesn't act like I would have guessed. He's so down to earth. He's so humble."

"Him?" I asked shocked.

"Yeah. Why?" she replied as if she had no clue what I was talking about.

"Nothing. I'm glad you got everything straighten out with your home."

"It's a true blessing," she said before moving on to someone else.

This was becoming crazy. I knew who Laine was. I had known who he was for the past fourteen years. He was not the generous, charitable guy who everyone thought he was. He was self-involved and only interested in what he could take from others. And I was ready to tell him that the next time I saw him.

The next time I saw him wouldn't be that night, though. He had stayed for a few minutes and then had left. I would need to wait until he showed up uninvited again. According to his declaration, that was going to be within another week.

For the next week, I found myself searching every crowd for him. He wasn't there. Every new person who entered my view, every moving object out of the corner of my eye, I wanted it to be him.

As the seven days passed, I found myself disappointed that he wasn't showing up. Hadn't he said that he would remind me every week? Sure, attending the funeral would definitely count as one, but was that all his word was worth?

It was as Jules and I socialized in front of Stuart's that we heard there was about to be a big announcement. To everyone's surprise, Bimini's Member of Parliament was also there. Seeing him, Jules and I had a feeling about what the announcement could be.

Whereas running water was quickly restored to the island after the hurricane, electricity wasn't. It had been ten weeks. And although free generators had been handed out as readily as food, it would be nice to no longer have to hear the constant drone of a running engine all day and night.

"Is that him?" Jules asked pointing at the man in front of the conch stand… with her other hand firmly clasping mine.

"Yeah, that's him," I told her as we repositioned ourselves to listen to what Minister Pindling had to say.

"Hello, my fellow Biminians," he said drawing polite applause from the crowd. "It has been a long hard road since Hurricane Betty. But, we stuck together, we offered our hand to each other when we needed help, and food when we were hungry. Today we have a landmark day when it comes to the recovery. Since we've waited too long already, I won't make you wait even more.

"Ladies and gentlemen, I'm happy to say that, as of today, Bimini again has power."

As he lifted his arms, newly hung lights lit the streets. Everyone cheered. It brought to light another thing that I hadn't noticed until then, the parking lot, the street and everywhere else was free of sand and debris.

With my nose pressed onto a tree trunk every day, I had missed the forest growing up around me. Life on Bimini was returning to normal. That was wonderful, but I couldn't deny the sinking feeling it gave me wondering what that meant for me.

I was still living in the temporary shelter while others returned to their repaired homes. My home was still rubble. I had no home to go back to and in spite of holding Jules's hand now, I had no one to go home with.

"How great is that?" the minister said as the cheers died down. "And we couldn't do this without our numerous international friends. One of which was particularly helpful for this endeavor, having not only paid for the island's new 50-megawatt generator, but having paid to have it delivered, and installed.

"I would like everyone to put your hands together for someone we are all very grateful for…"

"Oh no," I said seeing where this was going.

"Mr. Laine Toros," the minister said drawing Laine from the crowd. "Mr. Toros, would you like to say a few words?"

"Yes, thank you," Laine said emerging from the crowd.

"Oh no!" I repeated starting to sweat.

"What?" Jules asked still holding my hand.

"It's Laine. He's gonna…"

"What?"

"Thank you, Minister Pindling. It's been my honor to do what I can to help this community get back on its feet again. I saw what you were before the hurricane. I experienced the hurricane like you did, and I have been moved by the way everyone here has persevered in what might be the darkest of times.

"But honestly, I'm not sure how much credit I deserve for the assistance I've been giving. This wasn't my home… even though since coming here you all have made me feel at home and have given me a sense of belonging that I have been missing for a long time.

"No, I'm not sure how much credit I deserve. With all sincerity, I think that the true credit for what I have done should be given to one of you. He was the one who showed me to look past myself… for once, and to figure out what someone else needs.

"I would like everyone to put their hands together for someone I care tremendously about. I don't want to embarrass him by calling him out. But, you know who you are. I love you and I'm not going anywhere.

"Can everyone join me in giving him a round of applause?"

Everyone in the square applauded. They were applauding me. This wasn't right. None of this was right. I had to put an end to this. I had to show everyone who he really was.

"No, everyone. Stop! You have to stop. This man isn't who he's pretending to be."

"Reed, what are you doing?" Jules asked nervously.

I pulled my hand from hers and marched towards Laine and the Minister.

"You can't believe him. He's tricking all of you. You all think you know who he is, but you don't. I know this man. I've known him for a long time. He's selfish, self-involved, and he doesn't do anything unless it benefits him personally. You all are probably just a big tax write off for him."

Laine, who was now at my side, spoke up.

"Not that it matters, but that's not the way tax write-offs work. You have to spend the money with a charity based within the US to write it off. And considering my line of work, I couldn't write off a power generator."

"Okay. Then, he's doing it to manipulate you. He's just manipulating you like he manipulated me in the past and is trying to again."

"Who are you, young man?" the minister asked growing short of patience.

I looked at the Minister and then I looked at Laine. I didn't want to say it but I had to tell them.

"I'm that guy. I'm the guy he had you all applaud. And I can tell you from experience, you can't trust him."

"And why is that?" the minister asked angrily.

"Because I trusted him and it destroyed me," I told him feeling the wall I had put up around my heart slowly crumble.

"Listen here, young man, I have put up with enough from you…"

"No, Minister Pindling. Let him speak. He's right. I deserve it. He knows me well, probably better than anyone. I wasn't always good to him. I lied and tried to manipulate him. I couldn't see past my own selfish desires. It's true.

"But, as the man who knows me more than anyone in the world, tell me, Reed, is it possible that everything I've ever done, I've done because I love you? Sure, I often went about it the wrong way. I did things that hurt others and largely benefitted myself.

"But, go back to the beginning, the very beginning with us and ask yourself, "is it possible that everything I did, I did because I loved you." Because I do. Reed, I love you. I love you more than I have loved anyone in my life, and more than I ever will.

"I told you before that I'm not going anywhere. My heart is yours from now to the end of time. I…"

And that is when I kissed him. In front of everyone, I kissed him. I would like to say that it was to shut him up, but it wasn't.

I couldn't deny it anymore. I loved him too. I had always loved him and was always going to.

As the two of us locked lips, I heard a slow build of applause. First it was one person and then two. Soon the entire crowd was cheering and whistling. It was louder than I had ever heard them cheer before. People were catcalling and screaming. We were being bathed in the crowd's warm embrace and it filled a hole in my heart that led directly to my soul.

When I finally let go of Laine and looked at him, I realized something. For years I had thought that I had found my home on this island. I was wrong. I didn't know what home meant until that moment as I stared into Laine's eyes. I was at home in his eyes and I never wanted to be anywhere else again.

Taking his hand, I turned back to the crowd. They were still cheering. It brought me to tears. Leading Laine away, I knew where I wanted to be. It wasn't there in front of everybody. It was standing in front of the only other person who mattered.

Chapter 8

Jules

Well, goddamn! Because what else do you say after watching the man you love kiss another man in front of everyone? As Reed dragged Laine into the crowd, I wondered where they were going. Turns out, they were headed towards me.

"We should get out of here," Reed said to me with joyful tears in his eyes.

"Yeah, that's probably best," I told him before he took my hand and dragged the both of us away.

As we walked under the new lights that had been strung above the street, I looked over at Laine who caught my gaze and smiled back.

"So, I take it that you two made up?" Reed asked me.

"I forgave him for everything a long time ago," I told Reed. "In fact, I kinda thank him for it."

"You thank him?" Reed asked amused.

"Yeah. Whatever Laine's motivation was, it got me and my mother out of debt and it brought you back into my life. What else could have done that other than some crazy scheme?"

Reed laughed. "Yeah, I guess. Laine, you're forgiven," Reed told him making it clear in case the kiss hadn't already done that.

"Okay, I guess I'll ask," I said speaking up. "What now? Are the three of us a thing?"

"I think we're a thing," Laine volunteered. "I know I love him and, Jules, I can't imagine my life without you in it. I've become who I am because of you… and him. How could I live my life without both of you?"

I thought about it. "Yeah, I agree. Your life wouldn't be complete without me," I said with a smile. Laine laughed. "But seriously, as much as I love Reed is as much as I care about you, Laine. You are the most interesting person I have ever met. And, if I could, I would like to spend the rest of my life getting to know you."

"That sounds like love to me," Reed volunteered.

I thought about it for a second. "Yeah, I guess it does." I stopped the group, stepped in front of Reed and kissed Laine… hard. When our tongues had become properly acquainted, I leaned away and touched my lips. I felt light-headed and definitely wanted to do that again.

"So, is there somewhere we can go?" I asked feeling the flesh between my legs tingle.

"Well, I'm still sleeping at the shelter. You live with five other people and he's sleeping on a cargo ship," Reed pointed out.

"Those aren't exactly all of our options," Laine said with a smile.

"Where else is there?" Reed asked.

"Okay, you might have to forgive me for one more thing," Laine said. "I had an idea, and then ran with it. I might have gotten carried away."

"Oookaaay," Reed said nervously.

"I'll just show you. Just remember how much you love me. By the way, you do love me, right? I don't think you said it."

"I guess it'll depend on what happens next."

"Oh crap! No pressure. I'll just show it to you. Crap!" Laine said genuinely unnerved.

Laine led us on a 20-minute walk and then a ferry ride to South Bimini Island. Walking from there, Reed seemed to know where we were going and it made him more nervous.

When we got there, I still wasn't sure what we were supposed to be seeing.

"This is Reed's house," I said pointing out the obvious.

"Yes," Laine confirmed.

"Did you paint it or something?" I asked not sure what had changed.

I turned to Reed to see if he knew and found him staring at the building with tears rolling down his cheeks. Without a word, he turned to Laine and kissed him again. I still didn't see what was different. Although perhaps a little cleaner, it looked exactly the same as I remembered it, which was weird because I could have sworn that Reed had told me that his home had been razed to rubble.

When I entered Reed's place and saw that everything inside was new, I finally understood. The place had been destroyed. Laine had returned it to exactly what it was before the hurricane.

"I wanted to make sure you knew that I loved and respected you for who you are. I don't need you to change for me. I'll change for you," Laine told Reed.

"I love you, Laine. I always have, and always will," Reed responded before kissing him again.

Reed flicked a switch and the ceiling light turned on.

"Electricity," Reed said excitedly.

"Unfortunately, there's just water and power right now. In fact, you can say that all there is a floor and a bed," Laine said with a smile.

"There's a bed?" Reed asked headed to the bedroom.

"There's a bed," Laine confirmed.

After Reed left the two of us behind, Laine took my hand and walked me to the bedroom. When we got there, Reed was sitting on the bed. I ended up sitting next to him with Laine on my other side.

I turned looking at each of them before placing my hand on either of their legs. They both stared at me pleased and I felt like a kid in a candy store. Which one would I sample first?

Since he was the man of the hour, I chose Laine. Tilting my head back I gave him a kiss. It was the sequel to the kiss I had given him in the street under the lights. It was better than the original.

Laine was the first to begin to undress me, but not by much. Slipping his hand into my bra, he massaged my breast before removing my underwear. The warmth of his palm and the strength in his hand sent a warm pulse through my body. I wanted more of it. So when Reed then removed my pants and slid me up the bed, I was more than ready.

Lying naked beneath them, Laine took hold of my breasts as Reed spread my legs. Reed touched his nose to my swollen clit. It shot a tingle through me. He teased me like that until my engorged lips begged him for more. That was when his tongue took over driving me wild. First flicking my tip and then pressing it hard, I didn't know how long I would last.

The answer was not long. My pussy yearned for him. With Laine's tongue twirling around mine, I lost myself. And, bathed in the heat of my two guys, my legs clamped around Reed's head as he drove my orgasm home.

"Ehhhh!" I squealed feeling the rush of pleasure rip through me.

My legs danced as I lost myself in the moment. Reed wouldn't stop though, and the more he pressed, the more I was sure I would cum again.

Freeing myself of Laine, I gripped the sheets and heaved my naked chest into the air. Reed's caress was too much but I didn't want him to stop. Soon I couldn't control myself. My body was thrashing from one side to the next trying to consume the pleasure. I screamed wildly. I opened my eyes with the intention of begging him to stop when I caught a glimpse at what was going on with them.

With Reed's head buried in my pussy and his ass in the air, Laine had pulled down Reed's pants and had positioned his incredibly thick cock on his lover's hole. I could tell the moment Laine pushed it into Reed because Reed's tongue stopped. Immediately I grabbed the back of his head and forced him to continue. He did, and as he did, I watched Laine fuck the hell out of him.

The sight of them spiraled me into orgasm. It was the break Reed needed to moan and scream. My body was twitching violently. I couldn't stop it. Watching them was as good as any dick I'd ever had. And when

Reed grabbed onto me about to explode in orgasm, I squirted all over him unable to hold out any longer.

Squirting more than I had ever in my life, it was almost a relief when Reed rolled off of me. I say almost because it allowed one more thing that would make my night.

After a quick clean off, I watched Laine approach me with his cock still brick hard. For so long I had wondered what it would feel like to be fucked by him. Not only was his cock the longest I had ever seen, but it was also the thickest. I was drunk with passion by the time he took his rightful place on top of me. When he pushed himself into my slippery insides, I learned that Laine was worth the wait.

Laine filled me completely. His thickness touched every inch of me. As he thrust in and pulled out, it sucked me into a dream state. I don't know how long I was there, but upon the world's release, I saw my guy's face contort as he came.

I was pleased. Not only because I was with the two best guys on the planet, but because I knew that this was the way it was going to be ever after. I loved Reed and Laine, and they loved me. And as the two of them fell by my side and held me, the warmth of their strong, built bodies slowly lulled me to sleep.

Epilogue

Laine

Still spinning from what had to be the greatest sex of my life, I laid by Jules's side thinking about how lucky I was. I was about to tell Jules that when I heard her snore. It made me chuckle. Reed chuckled too.

Knowing he was awake, I found his hand as it rested on Jules's stomach. I interlocked my fingers with his. I could have stayed like that forever.

It was then that a thought hit me.

"Reed, do you remember that thing you told me about family."

"Oh, I hope it wasn't bad."

I chuckled. "I'm referring to when you talked about how important family was to you."

"Yeah, I remember that."

"Well, I think we should be a family."

"We already are," Reed said to my delight.

"I agree. But, what I meant to say was that I think we should have a family."

"Laine, you want kids?" he said with a laugh.

"No, I don't just want kids. I want your kids. I want Jules's kids."

"Then we'll have kids," Reed replied pleased.

"I still don't think you're understanding what I'm saying. I'm saying that I think that we should have kids. You and me… and Jules, of course."

"You mean you want the two of us to have kids? I'm not sure you understand how human reproduction works, Laine."

"Well, it just so happens I know someone who might be able to help us with that."

"With the two of us having a baby?" Reed asked confused.

"Yeah."

"Who? And, how would something like that even work?" he asked, still confused but with building excitement.

I smiled and squeezed Reed's hand. Those were great questions, but they were questions for tomorrow. Tonight I wanted to savor the beginning of the life I had always dreamed of having. I was with the two people I loved more than life. And, for that, I was eternally grateful.

The end.

**Keep reading for a sneak preview of 'Burning Blaze', the next book in the 'Taming the Beast' series. 'Burning

Blaze' is a standalone with a new steamy storyline, but it also includes what happens next with Laine, Reed, and Jules.

Burning Blaze

Chapter 1

Blaze

Did you ever have a night where you couldn't believe your luck? You're having one of the greatest times of your life and you feel on top of the world? But then when the night ends, you think it has ended, but no, it lingers. That great night sticks around and as fun as it was while it was happening, living with it day after day isn't as fun?

Let me tell you about my night like that. It started with me getting back into town and feeling as horny as fuck, excuse my language. So, what do I do? What I usually do. I call up a few friends and tell them to tell their friends that I'm throwing a party.

On the night, my penthouse is jumpin'. There are beautiful women for as far as your eyes can see and everyone is having a great time because of me. Circling the place I'm deciding who I want for the night, 'No, not her. No, not her. Oh, but how about them?'

At the bar next to the DJ booth, I spotted a set of girls who had to be twins. I get hard just looking at them. I decide that I want them both, which would be hard to get, even for me. But I head over to them and see what's possible.

"Your glasses look empty. What are you drinking?" I asked them.

"Water," one of them says in a very hot accent.

"Water? What are you doing? You can get whatever you want. Wait, are you two mermaids?"

The two girls look at each other confused. But they had to find it amusing because they started smiling. When they turned back to me I said,

"Mermaids. You don't know mermaids?"

The closest one to me shook her head, no.

"They're incredibly beautiful women, who live in the ocean. They have fish tales instead of feet except when they're on land. But then they have to keep drinking water?"

I wasn't sure if I was getting the legend right, but it was right enough because they got it.

"Ahh, mermaids!" They giggled. "No, we are not mermaids."

"Are you sure because I would definitely swim to my grave chasing after you two."

The girls laughed.

"I'm sorry, what's your names?"

"I'm Kaitlyn and this is my sister Katia," the more attractive identical twin said.

"Nice to meet you. I'm Blaze. Are you enjoying the party?"

Kaitlyn shrugged unimpressed.

"Really?" I asked surprised by her bluntness. European women. Am I right? "You know why you're not having fun?"

"Why?" Kaitlyn asked.

I pointed to her glass. "Water."

They both smiled knowing I was right. "We don't drink," Kaitlyn says.

That should have been my first warning sign. But, what can I say, they were beautiful, so I didn't listen.

"You know why you don't drink? It's because you've never tried a 1982 Dom Perignon."

Kaitlyn chuckled. "Really?"

"It will change your life," I told them feeling very confident.

"Where do we get some of this Dom Perignon?"

"Follow me to my wine room. I'll show you what true pleasure is."

"Is this your place?" Katia asked finally showing some interest.

"It is. Want a tour?"

After giving them a taste of the bubbly and showing them around, they were a lot more into what was going on. I know what had to come next. I had to let them think about what they saw and enjoy the rest of their drink. My penthouse was designed to get women into the one room I hadn't show them, my bedroom. But you had to take things slow with women like them. And sometimes, you even needed a little help.

Leaving them to wonder, I made sure they saw me talking to a few other women. I saw them staring. They could barely take their eyes off of me until at some point they got bored of it and disappeared onto the balcony.

Clearly, they were going to be tough nuts to crack, which is why when I saw Laine Toros enter and grab himself a drink, I nearly got hard. Laine was the ultimate wingman. The man was almost as good looking as me with a few billion dollars under management. More than that, he could get a woman naked faster than a gyno. The man had skills.

Bringing Laine in on the hunt was exactly want I had needed. Minutes later the twins were in my bedroom dropping their dresses in unison. When Laine told his girl to focus on me, I thought I was in heaven. I was getting exactly what I needed. I had a set of twins all over my jock and I was loving it.

The problem came when Laine suddenly took off. Yeah, that left me both twins, but two girls are hard to keep track of. At one point both were underneath me as I was rockin' their world. Then the second one came and I again focused on the first. I thought I was safe. How wrong was I?

When I was again drilling Kaitlyn, apparently Katia retrieved her purse and took out her phone. I didn't see it until the camera was squarely pointed at me. Did I stop right then like any sane man would have? Of course not. I have an unhealthy relationship with being recorded. I love it. So, seeing the camera, I took hold of the Swedish sisters and really went to work.

I would like to say that I made sure that you couldn't see my face in the video before they left. I would like to say that. But, I'm not gonna lie. I didn't. Who would have anticipated the girls' desire to be famous? I tell ya, Kim Kardashian has ruined the innocent pleasure of making a sex tape for everyone.

The girls could at least have been polite enough to blackmail me. Were they? No. As far as I could tell, they didn't even sell it to a distributor for cash. They just put it on the internet for the whole world to see.

Am I embarrassed by a video of me looking like an absolute stud living out every man's fantasy? No. Katia captured some good angles. Her camera work was on point.

No, the problem is that I'm not a 25-year-old NFL running back anymore. I am the CEO of a publicly held biotech company with assholes on the board. Shareholders were never happy when their CEO popped up on TMZ with a sex tape, no matter how hung they looked in it. The stuffed-shirts were crazy like that. Corporate life, am I right?

"Mr. Turner, the board will see you now," the receptionist said ushering me in.

I gotta say, knowing that everyone I knew had seen the video was quite a rush. The receptionist who had just spoken to me had seen it. I could tell by the way she looked at me. Before her, the security guard had seen it. There wasn't anyone I passed on the street that hadn't seen it. And, God did that feel good.

"Blaze, we're going to need you to resign as CEO."

"I'm sorry, what?" I asked sure I hadn't heard what I thought I had.

I looked around the conference table into each of the men's eyes. What the hell was happening?

"I'm not resigning as CEO. This is my company and I'm the largest shareholder."

"You're the largest individual shareholder. But, you only hold 49% of the voting shares. The rest of us hold 51%," Charles, the grey-haired lead asshole said.

"Yeah, but that would mean that every single one of you would have to vote to remove me. There is no way everyone thinks this is a good idea… could you?"

I scanned all of the faces and they stared me in the eyes except for one person, Dillion. He was the ex-teammate I gave 1% of the company to for the sole purpose of having my back. That bastard betrayed me too.

"Look, Blaze, you've embarrassed the company before and once again the company stock is in freefall."

Is it? I didn't see that. Crap, this *is* serious.

"The market just doesn't see you as stable. Blaze, it's not that we don't like you. You founded this company. You're the face of it. But the problem is that you are the face of it. This little stunt of yours has cost us a billion dollars in valuation. That's billion with a 'B', Blaze. We can't just do nothing. The board has to act. And now, you have to resign," Charles explained like the heartless prick he was.

It was at this point that I had to ask myself if the night with the twins was worth it. I know, the answer should have been obvious, but you weren't there. It was pretty fuckin' hot. I refer you to the video.

"I'm not gonna resign," I told Charles and the rest of them.

"We're not giving you another option," Charles challenged.

It was around that point when the receptionist entered the room and whispered something into Charles' ear.

"Put it up," he told her giving me time to think up the greatest comeback ever.

"I'm not resigning because... Let me tell you. I'm not resigning because... Because..."

"…Blaze Turner and I are engaged," a voice from the TV said.

Wait, I'm Blaze Turner, I thought before shifting my attention to the TV. I recognized the woman saying it. Her name was Ariel Katt. She was the CEO of Vermagin, a rival biotech company, and a world-class pill.

The last time I was in the same room as her, we got into an argument that turned into a food fight and $50,000 worth of damage to a hotel conference room. Like I said she was a real pill. And she was tough to swallow.

That made it even stranger that she was now on TV having what looked like a press conference about being engaged to some a guy named Blaze Turner. How many Blaze Turners were there?

"Blaze and my engagement might come as a surprise to some of you. A few of you might even be shocked. But I can assure you it's true. It was only because of our respective jobs that we decided to keep it quiet.

"In light of the released video, we can't keep it quiet anymore. Yes, this does not make me look good. Yes, Blaze Turner has cheated on me. But as the wise Tammy Wynette once said, if you love him, you will forgive him. I do love Blaze Turner. So, I will be standing by my man."

What the fu…

company, Blaze stole their patent and made billions from it leaving Quin with nearly nothing.

Why would Quin agree to such an arrangement? Because Quin was secretly in love with him. But Blaze screwed him, not in the good way, and tricked Quin into signing a contract that forced him to act buddy-buddy with Blaze in public. Truth was, though, that Quin wanted nothing but to see Blaze burn in hell.

So, now that Quin has invented something that is guaranteed to change all of humanity, and he again has the upper hand, what will he do when Blaze inevitable comes calling? Get his revenge, that's what. That is as long as his suppressed feelings for Blaze doesn't resurface.

'Burning Blaze' is a steamy bisexual romance with as many laughs as twists and turns. Loaded with enough MM, MFM, and MMF scenes to make your toes curl, it will leave you satisfied with its not-to-be-missed HEA ending.

*'Burning Blaze' is a standalone which includes appearances of the characters from 'Hurricane Laine'.

*****

Burning Blaze

I would like to say that I made sure that you couldn't see my face in the video before they left. I would like to say that. But, I'm not gonna lie. I didn't. Who would have anticipated the girls' desire to be famous? I tell ya, Kim Kardashian has ruined the innocent pleasure of making a sex tape for everyone.

The girls could at least have been polite enough to blackmail me. Were they? No. As far as I could tell, they didn't even sell it to a distributor for cash. They just put it on the internet for the whole world to see.

Am I embarrassed by a video of me looking like an absolute stud living out every man's fantasy? No. Katia captured some good angles. Her camera work was on point.

No, the problem is that I'm not a 25-year-old NFL running back anymore. I am the CEO of a publicly held biotech company with assholes on the board. Shareholders were never happy when their CEO popped up on TMZ with a sex tape, no matter how hung they looked in it. The stuffed-shirts were crazy like that. Corporate life, am I right?

"Mr. Turner, the board will see you now," the receptionist said ushering me in.

I gotta say, knowing that everyone I knew had seen the video was quite a rush. The receptionist who had just spoken to me had seen it. I could tell by the way she looked at me. Before her, the security guard had seen it. There wasn't anyone I passed on the street that hadn't seen it. And, God did that feel good.

"Blaze, we're going to need you to resign as CEO."

"I'm sorry, what?" I asked sure I hadn't heard what I thought I had.

I looked around the conference table into each of the men's eyes. What the hell was happening?

"I'm not resigning as CEO. This is my company and I'm the largest shareholder."

"You're the largest individual shareholder. But, you only hold 49% of the voting shares. The rest of us hold 51%," Charles, the grey-haired lead asshole said.

"Yeah, but that would mean that every single one of you would have to vote to remove me. There is no way all of you think this is a good idea… could you?"

I scanned all of the faces and they all stared me in the eyes except for one person, Dillion. He was the ex-teammate I gave 1% of the company to for the sole purpose of having my back. That bastard betrayed me too.

"Look, Blaze, you've embarrassed the company before and once again the company stock is in freefall."

Is it? I didn't see that. Crap, this *is* serious.

"The market just doesn't see you as stable. Blaze, it's not that we don't like you. You founded this company. You're the face of it. But the problem is that you are the face of it. This little stunt of yours has cost us a billion dollars in valuation. That's billion with a 'B', Blaze. We can't just do nothing. The board has to act. And now, you have to resign," Charles explained like the heartless prick he was.

It was at this point that I had to ask if the night with the twins was worth it. I know, the answer should be obvious, but you weren't there. It was pretty fuckin' hot. I refer you to the video.

"I'm not gonna resign," I told Charles and the rest of them.

"We're not giving you another option," Charles challenged.

It was around that point when the receptionist entered the room and whispered something into Charles' ear.

"Put it up," he told her giving me time to think up the greatest comeback ever.

"I'm not resigning because… Let me tell you. I'm not resigning because… Because…"

"…Blaze Turner and I are engaged," a voice from the TV said.

Wait, I'm Blaze Tuner, I thought before shifting my attention to the TV. I recognized the woman saying it. Her name was Ariel Katt. She was the CEO of Vermagin, a rival biotech company, and a world-class pill. The last time I was in the same room as her, we got into an argument that turned into a food fight and $50,000 worth of damage to a hotel conference room. Like I said she was a real pill. And she was tough to swallow.
Read more now

Sneak Peek:
Enjoy this Sneak Peek of 'Reckless Vandal':

Reckless Vandal
(MMF Bisexual Romance)
By
Alex McAnders

A bad boy billionaire, his good-hearted best friend, and the curvy woman of their dreams fall into an unforgettable MMF bisexual romance when a fake relationship leads to, friends becoming lovers, sizzling encounters, and longtime best friends giving in to their heart-aching passion.

HART
When Hart saw two of his kindergarten students teasing another, he stepped in. When he found out that the kid was being teased because he had two dads, Hart had the kid's imagine how they would treat him, their teacher, if Hart had a husband. Who would have known that one of the kids would misinterpret it and tell his conservative parents… who would then complain to the

school's conservative board… who would then go to his principal to get Hart fired?

Luckily the principle put her own job on the line to protect his. And all Hart has to do to save both of their jobs is to invite his "respectable" husband to meet the school board. Too bad Hart doesn't have a husband and the only one he had who would pretend was Vandal, his reckless childhood friend with more money than sense.

IVY
As principal, Ivy was surprised to learn that her favorite kindergarten teacher had a husband. Hadn't their night out together been a date? No matter, she wasn't going to allow the school's board to fire him just because he was gay.

But, the question was, how was her heart-thumping work-crush married to her drool-worthy celebrity crush, Vandal Scott. And when the three of them are forced together by a school retreat and the bad boy billionaire makes things complicated, what is Ivy supposed to do considering how tired she is of having more respectability than sex?

VANDAL
It's hard being drop dead gorgeous and born filthy rich, but Vandal Scott struggled through. But, seriously, what was genuinely hard was the boredom. So, when his childhood best friend asks him to play the role of his dutiful husband, Vandal throws himself into the part.

Who would have guessed that his pretend relationship would spark real feelings? And that the object of his affection would already have feelings for a beautiful principal who was a much better match for Hart than Vandal was?

Falling in love for the first time and having a billion dollars at his disposal, how will Vandal win the heart of his long time best friend? Desperate to have the life he didn't even know he wanted, how many lives was Vandal willing to wreck to get it?

'Reckless Vandal' is a steamy bisexual romance with as many laughs as twists and turns. Loaded with enough MM, MFM, and MMF scenes to make your toes curl, it will leave you satisfied with its not-to-be-missed HEA ending.

* Reckless Vandal' is a standalone which includes appearances of the characters from 'Hurricane Laine' and 'Burning Blaze'.

*****

Reckless Vandal

I don't know if it was the alcohol or his admission of young love, but staring into his soulful eyes, all I wanted to do was kiss him. I was losing my breath. The room became very hot. And as the moment dragged me closer to him on the couch, he leaned forward, slipped his hand around the nape of my neck and pulled my lips to his.

He kissed me like I wanted him to. His large hand had a strong hold of me and his body heat enveloped mine. Pulling my lips apart, his tongue entered my mouth. Finding my tip, the two touched. The sensation made my brain tingle. I needed more of him. And when our two tongues twirled around each other, I only wanted more.

Putting my drink down, I grabbed his body pressing it against mine. He felt so good on me. I dug my fingers into his back trying to pull him into my body. That wasn't enough. The smell of him was intoxicating. I needed his clothes off of him. And as I gripped his shirt and tore at it, he pulled from my lips and stared me in the eyes.

"Do you want to do this?" He asked me making me want him more.

"Yes," I purred.

"Then come," he told me before getting up from the couch and leading me to his bedroom.

Standing at the foot of his bed I stared at him. He moved slowly. Unbuttoning his shirt, he let it drop to the floor. His muscles rippled under the city's lights. The man was beautiful. I had missed touching him so much. And when he stepped forward and slowly undressed me, my cock grew hard. Not stopping with my shirt, he pushed his palm over my bulge and took hold.
Read more now

*****

Subscribe to my author YouTube channel 'Bisexual Romance Author Vlog' and get behind the scenes secrets about my stories and a personal look at my life as bisexual writing sexy romance novels:

What to expect?
- Book Secrets
- My Bi Life
- Romance & Sex Stories

BISEXUAL ROMANCE AUTHOR VLOG

www.ingramcontent.com/pod-product-compliance
Ingram Content Group UK Ltd.
Pitfield, Milton Keynes, MK11 3LW, UK
UKHW030657270525
6096UKWH00042B/704

9 781087 970387